COWBOYS & STARLIGHT

A STARLIGHT SWEET ROMANCE

JACQUELINE WINTERS

Cowboys & Starlight is a work of fiction. Names, characters, businesses, places, events, and incidents are either the products of the author's imagination or used in a fictitious manner. Any resemblance to actual persons, living or dead, or actual events is purely coincidental.

Editor: EJ Runyon, Bridge to Story

Copy Editor: Brenda Letendre, Write Girl Editing Services

Cover Design: Victorine Lieske

Proofreading: Michelle Josette, www.mjbookeditor.com

CHAPTER 1

onnie

Ronnie Ross dug one knee into the back seat of her compact SUV and planted the opposite foot firmly on its frame. “I can do this.” Gripping the last box holding the remnants of her former life, she tried shimmying it free from its tight quarters.

Forgetting to sign her lease renewal had presented its own set of problems. But adding unemployment to the mix had forced Ronnie to condense her belongings in her car like Tetris pieces, wedging every box, container, and stuffed suitcase into its nooks and crannies.

The box of tile backsplash samples wouldn’t budge.

With a deep breath and a hard yank, her hands slipped from their cardboard handholds. Ronnie shot backwards onto the hard, gravelly surface. A rock stabbed painfully into her hamstring.

"Thanks for the warm welcome, Wyoming," she muttered to the small stretch of fourteen narrow storage units with orange steel doors, lined up in two rows, vacant of people or even wildlife now that the owner had left her alone with her rented space.

At the sound of a diesel engine, Ronnie quickly picked herself up and dusted off her jeans. She didn't want anyone to know she was here, hiding her pitiful failure of a life into an eight-by-eight unit.

The truck—white, not hunter green like her brother's—passed by the storage yard and sped out of town. Ronnie let out a breath.

Hudson was so proud of her for chasing her dreams. Had told her so only a few days ago on the phone. Deciding the one box of backsplash wouldn't spill her secret before she did, Ronnie yanked the door to her unit shut and clipped on a padlock. How humiliating would it be to break it to him that she'd just been fired? Picturing the pitiful look in his eyes nearly brought Ronnie to tears.

Where average people might stuff furniture, books, framed photos, or collections of DVDs in a storage unit, Ronnie's held cartons of samples. That was most of *her* life. Paint colors, carpet squares, fabric swatches, tile samples. Everything a well-prepared interior designer needed to someday be successful on her own.

Hopping back in her car, Ronnie turned up the only radio station she'd been able to find and crept along the drive to the road. The storage units were set up like some maze, not placed well. But for the price, she'd deal with the blind turns and lack of those convex mirrors mounted up high.

The hours she'd spent on the show had been grueling, working for an interior designer who found her fame on reality TV. The show, *Design of Your Dreams,* was an instant hit, and Ronnie'd been the lucky intern working for Lana Bojanski when fame followed. Though Ronnie had very little screen time, America seemed to love her witty personality. The producers insisted Lana hire her on as a full-time assistant.

Cringing, Ronnie wondered if the producers would decide to air the embarrassing episode of her being fired from that very job. Ronnie with her blouse misbuttoned, rushing to the celebrity client's house with her water-damaged cell phone lodged in a bowl of rice, grains flying free in her mad dash.

Ronnie couldn't call because her phone was waterlogged. Lana hadn't cared.

"I don't care if you overslept, if your phone died, if you had car trouble. You're over two hours late.

Didn't I say be on time or don't bother showing up at all?"

"I'll do whatever you need to make this right," she promised. But her pleading got her nowhere. There was no flicker of pity or understanding in Lana's fire-shooting eyes.

"Nothing you *can* do, Veronica." Lana's venomous sting still cut deep, a week after its bite. "You're fired."

It had been the final blow. No one ever called Ronnie by her given name except her mother when she was in trouble.

Weaving though the unit maze, the memory jarred, tears threatening once again. Hopefully, a couple of weeks here in Wyoming with Hudson would help Ronnie reset—figure out a way. She flipped off the radio, the station now mostly static. Whatever it took, she'd get her job back. Somehow.

The blare of a honking horn shook her from her daze. A long-bed silver pickup filled her driver's side window. She heard the crunch before she felt the collision.

Once the gentle rocking stopped, she shifted into park. Hands still anchored to the steering wheel, Ronnie slowed her breathing. The impact to her front bumper had seemed minimal, but with a truck that enormous, there had to be a decent dent.

When she saw a man come around the front of her car, she took a deep breath. Ronnie slid her sunglasses to the top of her head, glancing in the rearview mirror in search of any unwanted witnesses.

Ronnie pushed open her door, expecting an apology. The man staring back at her was filling out some Wranglers quite well, and she couldn't help but notice how his jeans rode low on his hips. For a moment, she wasn't even mad that her bumper was probably smashed. But the blue eyes peeking out from beneath the brim of his tan cowboy hat would have been a lot more attractive if they weren't filled with disbelief.

"Please tell me you weren't on your phone?" His deep voice held a light tone of reprimand, as if scolding a child.

Ronnie's skin prickled, her defenses flaring. Maybe she should've approached the blind corner a little slower, but she hadn't been *on her phone*. "It's hard to see around these things!" She waved her arm at the orange units. "And how do I know you weren't on *your* phone?" Ronnie walked a little closer to the impact site to assess the damage. Her car definitely sported a dent in the quarter panel. "Your monster truck dented my bumper."

His hands came up, revealing the lack of a ring, she noted. Not that she cared at all about that. He waved at his truck and then back to her. "*I* was just driving down the road."

Ronnie narrowed her eyes, assessing him and his

possible motives. Just motives. There was definitely no assessing how well he filled out that dark blue T-shirt.

The cowboy dipped down to examine the damage. "Just a small dent. Trent down at Anderson's can pop it out pretty quick. Local body shop. I'll give him a call. He owes me a favor."

"Where is that?" Ronnie figured in a town this small, she could zip over there to have it fixed before she met Hudson for dinner. The last thing she wanted was to explain why her little SUV had a fresh dent.

The cowboy nodded toward the setting sun. "Trent's closed up by now or I'd be heading there too."

"Your truck isn't even scratched!"

The tall cowboy knelt from the other side of the damage site. "There is too a scratch. You can't waltz into town and drive like you're still in the big city."

Before Ronnie could fire a retort, he started laughing. Ronnie narrowed her eyes at the menacing cowboy. "This is funny to you?"

"I was just making a . . . never mind. Look, I'm willing to overlook it this time. People drive slower around here and follow things like traffic laws."

"How did—"

"Your license plate doesn't help." He pointed, with what might be amusement dancing in his blue eyes. "Don't get a lot of folks from Illinois out this way. And you have 'city girl' written all over you. Especially with those shoes."

Ronnie looked down at her wedge sandals. "What's wrong with—"

"Nothing." The cowboy shook his head. "What are you doing in the storage unit yard anyway? Not moving to town, are you?"

"Of course not." A small tinge of panic rose, but she kept her glare steady. "I pulled in so I could use the GPS on my phone." The lie rolled off her tongue easily enough. Never mind that she only had one bar and her map feature wasn't cooperating. Starlight, Wyoming had fewer than twelve thousand people, Hudson had told her. How hard could it be to find a restaurant without a map?

"You couldn't have picked a better place for that?" He nodded toward a deserted gravel lot on the other side of the road, with no obstructions like the boxy units. "Like across the street?"

A car rolled up to their little accident scene, cautiously edging around them. The cowboy waved the driver on.

"Look, if you're done insulting me, I really need to go."

"Back to Chicago?"

"And my brother said this was such a welcoming town," Ronnie muttered under her breath. "If you'll kindly peel your bumper off my car, I'll get out of your hair." Ronnie dropped back into her car and slammed the door shut before she felt tempted to add any more insults. If she never saw this cowboy again, it'd be too soon.

CHAPTER 2

olten

Colten Livingston backed up his long-bed truck, dislodging his bumper from the compact SUV. Thankfully he'd been crawling along, watching a stray elk at the edge of the graveled lot to ensure it didn't make a mad dash across the street, or her bumper might be more than a little dented. The last thing he needed was a reason to talk to *that* woman again.

Colten recognized the type: city girl caught up in the idea of country living. First chance she got, she'd run back to civilization and all the conveniences—and shoe stores—she was used to.

It didn't stop him from catching a glimpse of her

leaning over the bumper, rubbing it with her hand as if it were a living thing. Her wavy ponytail, the color of dark chocolate, fell to her shoulder, shielding her face but showcasing what looked to be soft skin.

He did feel bad about the dent, but Trent would be able to pop it out in a couple of minutes. With any luck, the gesture would help the woman head out of town sooner rather than later. Trent owed Colten a favor for helping repair his grandfather's pasture fence a couple of weekends ago. Maybe he should have saved his favor. She hadn't even said thank you for his offer to have her dent repaired.

At the outskirts of town, just past the water tower sporting the town's name, *Starlight*, on its broad side, Colten slowed for the turn that would take him to his childhood home. The long, winding gravel drive snaked through a patch of cottonwood trees, healthier than most around here. When the driveway forked right, he stayed left. To the right sat an empty two-story barn, tucked into a cluster of trees. Years ago, there'd been horses. But once his dad got sick, his parents were forced to sell them.

He continued on through a clearing, to where a two-story structure sat atop a gentle hill. A fine house with a wraparound porch, though it was in desperate need of a paint job.

His mom, Becca Livingston, sat in one of two rockers on the front porch, nursing a cup of coffee. Colten's dog, Lou, sat at her feet and perked up at the sight of his truck approaching, her tail wagging against the wooden planks. He parked beside his mom's red Ford truck and hopped out. Before he made it to the steps, he felt her observant eyes studying his expression.

"Something crawl up your britches?"

Colten hopped up the three stairs, greeted by an excited Lou. Rubbing the pup behind the ears like she loved, he eyed the opposite rocker. His dad's seat. It didn't matter that he'd been gone four months. It didn't feel right to sit there. Probably never would. Instead, Colten dropped down on the porch, his feet stretched onto the stairs. Lou's tail batted up against his shoulder as she wriggled. "Nothing to worry about."

"You're scowling."

"I don't *scowl*."

"If you say so."

Two women under his skin in the same half an hour. That had to be a new record. Colten's mind kept drifting back to the storage unit lot, wondering what the city girl had been doing there. Why hadn't she pulled into the empty lot across the street without any obstructions?

"I told you I'll be gone for a week?" his mom said.

"Denver?"

"Yeah."

He knew what that meant. He'd need to watch the house. He'd been meaning to replace some of the trim in the dining room anyway. With no one underfoot, that seemed doable, but working on the Livingston ranch for his uncle kept him busy. He'd think on it. Mom hated to see him fuss over a house she'd eventually have to leave behind.

Two years ago, Colten moved back when his dad grew too weak and spent more time at doctors' offices and hospitals than home. He'd taken his dad's place working at the ranch.

But now that his cousin Jed was out of school for the summer, Colten might get Mom's trim replaced. Heck, with an entire week, he might get far enough on painting before she got back and stopped him.

"There's really no way to sugar coat this, Colten." She leaned forward in her chair to stop the rocking and hugged her hands around her mug. "It's time. I'm selling the house."

Colten tensed for a moment but relaxed almost instantly. They'd talked about this months before Dad passed, how when he was gone his mom would move on to Denver to be closer to the rest of her family. Somehow Colten believed she'd stick around for a couple of years.

"Going out to house hunt?"

"Yeah."

"How soon you looking to sell?" He had to stay objective or he'd lose it. Sometimes the sting of his dad's absence cut razor sharp, right to his chest. It was trying to now, but Colten swallowed it back. If he broke down, his mom surely would too.

"Well, need to get it ready first." She gestured to the siding. "Figure I'd hire someone to come out and help once I get back."

"I can do the work, Mom."

"No." She shook her head. Her wavy hair, pulled back in a low, loose ponytail, shook with it. Strands of silver glistened in the sunset against the fiery red sky. Colten didn't like seeing his mom age. It only reminded him how precious life was. That they'd lost his dad much too early.

"No?"

"This time of year the ranch'll keep you plenty busy. And you should be using your *spare* time to focus on your future. Make that phone call to your old boss and get working on making your way back to Glacier. Find out what recertifications you might need to get done."

They'd talked about this too. How he could get on with the life he left behind to come back. Well, the job he could go back to. Danica, she was long gone and could stay that way. "I can still work on the house," he offered.

He might have to redo paperwork that was now more than two years old, but the formalities wouldn't consume much of his time. His boss had been clear about hiring him back when he was ready. Colten had dreamed about those peaceful days roaming the mountainous acres since he left.

"I don't want you to end up stuck. Promise me while I'm gone you'll make that call."

"I chose to come back here. You remember that, right?" Lou perked up at the sight of a squirrel, her busy tail swishing against his arm.

"Lot of good it did you."

Colten didn't have much to say to that. It had cost him a lot, returning to Starlight. He'd been offered his dream position as a park ranger at Glacier National Park but only made it three months before Dad's diagnosis. Aggressive cancer. Moving home to Wyoming had cost him a wife, too.

But not moving back had never been an option. When Dad fell ill, chasing his dreams meant Colten wouldn't be around to say goodbye. As it was, his dad beat out the three-month odds he'd been given and hung on for fourteen more beyond that diagnosis. Though there'd been plenty of rough days, there had been some really good ones. Colten had been given memories of afternoons fishing. Of riding on the trails of the gently rolling hills talking about life. Not everyone was so lucky.

"You should let me help on the house," he said. "Hate to see some shoddy contractor mess her up."

"I'll think on it. Give me a bit. I'll be right out and we'll get going." Becca stood from her rocker and took her empty cup inside, letting Lou in with her.

When she returned, she'd changed the blouse she wore and the subject. "Hudson tell you what this special-occasion dinner is about?" Becca asked as they made their way to Colten's truck.

"Nope." He jingled his keys and shrugged. "Guess we'll find out."

CHAPTER 3

An upper deck wrapped around the front and one side of the Starlight Bar and Grill. Half a dozen people leaned against the railing, sipping on drinks. All in plaid shirts, half wore cowboy hats. "I don't belong here," Ronnie mumbled. The urge to run to her car and drive straight back to Chicago tugged at her. She was so out of her element.

Maybe coming here had been a mistake. How could she possibly get her job back if she hid out in some country town in the middle of nowhere? She barely had two bars on her phone. She should be back in Chicago, studying, learning, looking for new clients to bring the firm. With enough persistence, Lana would cave. She had to.

Of course, being homeless came with its own set of problems. It wasn't easy convincing a prospective landlord to rent to you without a job. But if she'd stayed in Chicago, sucked it up and moved back in with her parents for a few weeks, she wouldn't have to admit her biggest failure to Hudson tonight. Despite the urge to jet, she kept her feet moving forward past the last row of parked cars.

A sign overhead simply read *Bar*, so Ronnie followed a long wooden ramp to the upper level, where Hudson told her the restaurant would be.

Despite feeling out of place, the log cabin exterior intrigued her, making her curious about the theme. Her interior-design brain locked on, memories of leaving Chicago a faint whisper. How old was this building? How had it been constructed? Were the logs cut from nearby timber or had it been special ordered, quarter sawn?

Though Lana's clients primarily included luxury homeowners, most of their properties modern and sleek, Ronnie yearned to work with something older. Something with more character. What stories could these logs, the color of perfectly toasted marshmallows, tell?

"There's my famous little sister!" She heard the familiar voice, and searched till she found Hudson in the crowd. She'd missed him, one of those hidden beneath a black cowboy hat, leaning with a beer in hand. Setting the bottle on the thick wooden railing, he barreled toward her with outstretched arms. They clamped around Ronnie before she had a moment to prepare.

"I . . . uh—" Ronnie tapped him on the shoulder, but her brother only squeezed harder. "I can't breathe!" she spit out in a strangled whisper.

"Sorry!" Hudson let go, and the air came back. "I'm just excited to see you. It *has* been over two years, you know."

Ronnie saw no need to bring up why that was. "I'm excited to see you, too." The last time she saw Hudson, he'd been standing at the altar, waiting for a bride who never showed. Days after that let-down, he called to tell her he'd accepted a summer ranching job in Wyoming.

"Let's get something to eat." Hudson waved her farther inside. "Bet you're starved."

"You could say that." Ronnie'd spent two and a half days on the road, stopping long enough to sleep and refuel—both the car and her stomach. She'd eaten enough gas-station hot dogs to last a lifetime; it left her craving something hearty and filling.

Inside the rustic restaurant Ronnie found reclaimed wood tables, wagon wheel accents, and a stone fireplace along the far wall.

"The Starlight Bar and Grill is no fancy Chicago restaurant." Hudson steered her, hand on her shoulder, to a booth adjacent to the unlit fireplace. He hung his hat on a hook on the outside of the booth and slid in. "But the food's amazing."

The booth's leather creaked as she slid in. "I like it," Ronnie said. "It's got character." When she had time for meals out, it'd been to take notes while Lana consulted with clients. Those restaurants catered to the sleek, modern look Lana's clientele wanted in their homes.

Ronnie's designer eye couldn't help but absorb the character of the Starlight Bar and Grill. A single string of white lights danced along the walls, just above the windows, giving the dimly lit restaurant a true starlit effect. "Nice!"

"You're supposed to be on vacation," he teased. "But you can't turn it off, can you?"

Slipping a plastic-covered menu from behind the condiment tray, Ronnie shrugged in apology. "Hazard of the job, I guess." A job she no longer had.

Dread filled her chest. How was she going to tell him she'd messed up in such a huge way? Hudson had always been her biggest fan. Two weeks ago, she told him all about the promotion she was certain was coming her way. She'd gushed at the thought of being an interior designer. At no longer being *just* the assistant.

"How is work go—"

"Hudson Ross, who is this pretty lady?" Their waitress wore cowboy boots and a Western-style shirt. A friendly smile extended toward Ronnie, but the woman kept sneaking glances at Hudson.

"Patti, this is my little sister, Veronica."

Ronnie hated it when anyone called her that. It felt too formal and stiff. "Ronnie," she added.

"She's a famous designer from Chicago, gracing our little town with her presence for a couple of weeks." Pride beamed from that smile, and Ronnie felt her heart constrict. She should have tried harder, insisted they talk outside first. Now she'd have to eat, then dump her unfortunate news on him.

"Are you, now? That's interesting."

Ronnie pasted on a smile, returning her attention to the menu as though she needed to survey their water options.

"Been on TV, too." Hudson had always loved embarrassing her. Sometimes it was by teasing. Sometimes it was by bragging to others while she squirmed in her seat, unable to escape. But he had no idea this embarrassment wasn't modesty.

"I recognize you now!" Patti's eyes widened, her smile growing with them. "You're on that TV show. With that designer, Lana Bojanski."

Surely Ronnie was a shade of red to match the booth's leather by now, even if the low lighting hid some of it. "Don't mind my brother. He likes to brag." Ronnie tried to dismiss the unwanted attention. There'd been a few times in Chicago when someone recognized her and asked for a selfie to post online. Those times had always made Ronnie feel special, as though she was on the right track.

Now the recognition felt closer to a death sentence. Did people in this little town really watch Lana's show? How could she lay low if too many did?

"She's always been shy about the spotlight," Hudson explained, unrolling his silverware from its napkin and grinning.

"And I'm on *vacation,* as he keeps reminding me."

"Well, welcome to Starlight. Hope you enjoy our little town. It's no Chicago, but wait 'til you see the sky on a cloudless night. You'll understand what your brother loves about this place. We're sure glad he decided to stay."

They ordered their drinks and an appetizer, sending Patti on her way without any selfie requests, much to Ronnie's relief. "She knows your name?" Ronnie couldn't help but ask.

"That's the beauty of living in a small town. Lots of people know me by name."

"You're not planning on leaving, are you?"

"I like it here." Hudson shrugged. "Is that such a bad thing?"

"I'll let you know once I've had a chance to look around." Her words held a hint of jest and he smiled. It was refreshing to see him happy again. Ronnie wondered if maybe he'd met someone, but the question could wait.

"Give Starlight a little time," Hudson suggested. "It grows on you. I know you'll be going back to your fancy job, but I bet you'll want to come back and visit."

She should do it now, rip off the Band-Aid. But after all that business with Patti, Ronnie needed a moment to gather her thoughts. Her words. This humiliating news would surely shatter his good mood and crush that smile she hadn't seen since before the wedding. Ronnie didn't think she could endure that right now.

"Hey, I'm going to use the ladies' room."

"I can't promise to save you any soda bread. It's crazy good."

Normally Ronnie would fire back a witty remark, but her throat seemed swollen shut. Instead, she scurried off.

After locking the bathroom door behind her, thankful it was a one-person room, she faced herself in the mirror behind the door. She needed to get it together. The longer she put this off, the harder it would be. Part of her wanted to keep the truth hidden. If she could convince Lana to hire her back, maybe she wouldn't have to tell Hudson about the . . . snag.

But Ronnie'd always been a horrible liar when it came to her brother. If she didn't tell him now, the truth would come out in another more humiliating way. Especially if the producers decided to air that dismissal show ahead of schedule. She'd seen them do it before, when something exciting happened. They'd rearrange the schedule to boost ratings.

She leaned against the sink, ran some cool water over her hands first, then dabbed some on her red cheeks. She looked as if she'd been out in the sun too long. Thank goodness for that indirect lighting.

"Okay, Ronnie," she said into the mirror. "You can do this. It's going to suck, but get it over with." Sometimes mirror talk helped when she had to give Lana bad news about delays or setbacks. It didn't change the reaction she received, but it did help steel herself for circumstances created.

Ronnie marched back toward their booth, more than prepared to blurt out the news before she chickened out.

But the words caught in her throat. It wasn't only Hudson sitting there now. A woman about her mother's age sat next to him, engrossed in conversation. The woman smiled while they talked, and in the dim light Ronnie noticed lines creased at the outer edges of her eyes. Something about those lines hinted at a tough life and a strong-willed woman.

And there was a man sitting in Ronnie's spot, his tan cowboy hat hanging from a hook at the side of the booth.

"You must be Veronica." The cowboy slid out of

the booth, alluring blue eyes meeting her own. The smile nearly melted her into a puddle until recognition flared in his expression. "*You're* Hudson's little sister?"

"Ronnie." The word came out strangled, a failed attempt to sound civil warring with the snappy tone that tried to escape. She'd hoped to avoid this particular cowboy during her visit, but he'd somehow warranted an invitation to dinner. And he seemed *amused* by it, if that smirk was any indication. "I prefer Ronnie."

"Ronnie," he said flatly. "I'm Colten."

During the exchange, his eyes danced with humor. Would he keep quiet to avoid causing a scene? Or would he find enjoyment in embarrassing her in front of Hudson? Colten extended his hand. Ronnie had little choice but to take it, since it was offered with a pleasant, "Nice to finally meet you."

"Hudson talks about you all the time," the woman beside her brother added.

The dread from before intensified. *What had he told them?* She couldn't drop her news on Hudson now. Not in front of his friends. And certainly not in front of the irritating cowboy she crashed into. "Nice to meet you," Ronnie managed before retaking her seat. Colten slid into the booth after her. Her face flushed again, but this time for an entirely different reason.

"Ronnie," Hudson said. "This is Becca Livingston."

"I'm Colten's mom."

At least Ronnie had the sense to shake her hand. "A pleasure, Mrs. Livingston."

"She has manners." Becca smiled approvingly at Hudson. "I like that. Becca will be fine, though, hun."

"Hope you don't mind us crashing your dinner," Colten said. "Hudson insisted."

"Not at all." Her smile was forced, but at least there was a sweating glass of ice water on the table for Ronnie to sip on. This night was quickly going south. Not only would her news have to wait, but she and Hudson had so much to catch up on. Now that would have to wait, too.

"Hudson tells us you're a designer in Chicago," Becca directed at Ronnie. "What's that like, working for *the* Lana Bojanski? I absolutely love the show. I know my way around some power tools, but I'll admit I have about as much design sense as a cardboard box."

Ronnie could pretend that her life hadn't changed. Turn back the clock to one month ago when her life was looking on track and just about perfect. It was only through one dinner, right? "It's a little crazy," Ronnie started. "But I absolutely love it."

With drinks and appetizers delivered, everyone

reached in. She went on to regale them about her typical daily tasks—meetings with clients, forging relationships with retailers who offered unique products she could work into designs, putting out proverbial fires when things went wrong. "There are days I pretty much live on the jobsite, making sure everything goes with as few hitches as possible."

Hudson tipped his drink her way. "You forgot sleep."

Becca smiled, her teeth flashing as she pushed her plate aside in preparation for her entrée. Her eyes twinkled approval, and Ronnie finally relaxed. "You don't hear about all that on TV."

"There's a lot involved, and sometimes it feels like sleep will have to wait for a month we're not shooting," Ronnie said, then immediately added, "But it's so rewarding to see the look on the happy client's face when their vision comes to life. I know reality TV can be a little staged at times, but that's one part of the show that's authentic."

Becca poured a packet of sugar into her iced tea and stirred with her straw. "What about that episode where they showed you manning a table saw?"

Before Becca could ask, Colten jumped in, "Was that staged?" She felt Colten's intense gaze burning a spot in her cheek, but she ignored him as she flattened a napkin in her lap. He probably expected her to say it was. Impossible to grasp that a city girl could wield a power tool.

"Nope, that was real." Ronnie beamed with a pride.

"Ronnie's pretty handy with power tools," Hudson boasted.

She knew many designers who didn't even know how to work a power drill. But she'd made a point to learn every aspect she could. "I jump in if I can, if the contractors are running behind. We have a good crew on most projects, and they've been very willing to teach me to be useful." *After signing a bunch of waivers,* she thought but didn't add. "It comes in handy if you know your way around a circular saw or a tile cutter."

Ronnie should feel guilty about how easy it was pretending she was still a part of all that, but it allowed the humiliation to fade.

Becca asked, "What do you have planned for your vacation?"

"You know, I hadn't really thought of anything." Ronnie looked at Hudson, and they shared a smile. "I kind of sprang this trip on him. I don't think he was prepared to entertain me."

"I do have to work," Hudson admitted. "But I'll make some time to show her around when I can. Joe agreed to let me off by four most days."

"You don't strike me as a woman who likes to be idle too long." Becca studied her now, and Ronnie wasn't sure what to make of that. It wasn't a fierce look, but it felt intense.

Ronnie reached for her ice water and took a good gulp. "You're right. I do like to keep busy. I'm not great at this relaxing vacation thing."

"How'd you feel about a small project?"

Colten jumped in. "Mom, no."

Patti delivered their meals, interrupting the conversation. The aroma of her perfectly cooked ribeye made Ronnie's stomach rumble. She couldn't remember the last time she'd had a steak.

"She's on vacation," Colten continued once Patti left them. "Anything you need done at the house, I can take care of while you're gone. I already told you that."

Ronnie's interest piqued. The fact that Colten seemed instantly opposed made it almost a challenge now. "What kind of project?"

"My house is a bit outdated. While Colten's father was alive, we never put much into upgrades outside of appliances and the main bathroom. Everything went to the ranch." For the first time that evening, Becca dropped her eyes, staring blankly at the empty bread tin. "It has good bones. But the living and dining room need a facelift. Kitchen could use some help, too. Just basics. Flooring, maybe a coat of paint."

"Mom—"

"I own the house, Colten. I can hire someone if I want to." Becca turned back to Ronnie. "Too tired from traveling to stop by and see the place tonight?"

"She did drive for two straight days," Hudson said, offering her the chance to say no. "I talked her into coming down here first to get some decent food in her before I let her sleep."

"Why didn't you fly?" Colten asked.

"I like driving." Not entirely a lie. Given other options, though, Ronnie would've boarded a plane instead of driving. But with her future uncertain, she hadn't felt comfortable leaving her life packed in some city storage unit. She liked having her design materials close by.

"You know, since you're probably wiped, why don't you swing by in the morning, when you're rested?" Becca suggested. "I have to leave for Denver before lunch, but I think we can get all the details worked out before then."

"I can do that."

Becca smiled. "Gives me time to make a call. Confirm you're the real deal." There was a light edge to her words, but the woman meant business. "Can't trust everything we see on TV."

Now might be the best time to drop the bomb. If this charade went on any longer and Becca found out she'd been fired, it would make Hudson look like a fool. It was one thing for him to pity her unfortunate situation, but quite another to humiliate him in front of people important enough to him to warrant a dinner invitation.

CHAPTER 4

onnie

"Ronnie! It's good to hear your voice!" The sound of Reese's familiar voice brought relief. It was the first normal thing about her entire day. For a moment, Ronnie could pretend everything was as it'd always been. That she was calling Reese to beg a favor to find the last scrap of the perfect blue marbled fabric in Chicago for a bedroom remodel. Or the address of the man with the reclaimed barn-wood doors she needed for a home office design.

But this call was far from normal.

"Reese, how are you?"

"Girl, don't go changing the subject! Where are

you? I've been trying to get a hold of you for three days!"

Guilt crept up now. Reese, her only true friend, had been simply a call or text away since the incident. She even suggested Ronnie lay low for a couple of weeks and let Lana cool off. Let Ronnie's former boss navigate her incredibly packed days without her loyal assistant to realize how badly she needed her back. But Ronnie failed to mention any travel plans during Reese's last pep talk.

"Reese, where are you?" Ronnie asked cautiously, constant shuffling on the opposite end seeping through the phone. Reese wasn't one to sit still, which was odd when one considered she worked behind a desk.

"At home, working on a little side project. Lana tried to make half the office work until midnight, but we fled." When Ronnie didn't offer her usual crack in return, or immediately say anything, Reese added, "It's horrible what Lana did. Everyone thinks so. We all miss you." Another pause. "Is everything okay?"

How could Ronnie possibly beg this huge favor? The last thing she should be doing was tangling her only friend in her web of lies. "I'm in Wyoming."

"What?" The shriek on the other end forced Ronnie to pull the cell from her ear. "Wyoming! What on Earth are you doing all the way out in cowboy country?"

Ronnie cautiously poked her head out from the bedroom door of Hudson's very cozy cabin to ensure he hadn't come back from running an errand. She made her way into the cramped sitting area. "Visiting my brother. You're the one who suggested I lay low . . ."

"So, you'd do that best a thousand miles away?"

For the first time during their conversation, Ronnie cracked a smile. "Hudson's been trying to talk me into coming to see him since he moved out here."

"That was over two years ago!"

"Figured now was as good a time as any."

"What's the problem?"

Kicking off her shoes, Ronnie sank back into Hudson's mustard yellow recliner. It promptly tried swallowing her up whole. "I can't tell him yet."

"He's your brother, Ronnie. You really can't confide in him?"

"It's not that. It's just . . . he's so proud of me." Tears were threatening now. He'd been her biggest fan, encouraging her since she was little. Ronnie'd known she wanted to be an interior designer since she was eleven and her mom gave her free rein to decorate her bedroom however she wanted. "I was going to tell him. Really, I was, but—"

"Something happened."

"Yeah." Ronnie sighed. "Hudson invited a couple of friends to dinner. I couldn't drop news like that in front of his guests." The image of

Colten's amused eyes came back to her. Ronnie found herself rubbing her hand where the lingering sensation of his touch still had her puzzled. "Anyway, reason I'm calling is . . . it landed me a job. In Starlight."

"Ronnie, that's great! Don't you see?"

"Not exactly." Ronnie had to stop her friend before she got too carried away. "Becca Livingston, that's the client. Well, she's only *verbally* hired me. She won't make it official until she checks me out." Ronnie swallowed, a feeling like it was a hunk of slimy frog. "She's going to call the office tomorrow."

"What?"

"I hardly ever ask for personal favors. I feel horrible asking this one. But Reese, can you make sure you answer her call? Tell I still work there? I know it's horrible of me, but she was so excited that she recognized me from TV. She loves the show."

"This has bad idea written all over it," Reese warned, but she didn't say no outright.

"I know."

"In big, bold, blinking letters."

"I didn't want to embarrass Hudson in front of his friends. What could I do? I was going to tell him all about it—tonight. But if I can pull this little job off in two weeks, I can show Lana how capable I am of managing my own project. Use *that* to get my job back. I need this, Reese. Then I won't have to tell Hudson I screwed up."

"You're sure you can't get the job in Starlight on your own? You have your portfolio, right?"

"Becca Livingston, well, she seems like a tough client." Ronnie feared the woman's reaction if she found out all this was a lie. "The only validation she wants is that I'm really the assistant she saw on TV."

"I don't like this."

"I know."

"But . . . I'll do it."

"Thank you!" Ronnie tried to push out of the recliner, but the thing was determined to swallow her in its fluffy cushions. "You have no idea what this means to me, Reese. I'll work harder on this job than I've ever worked before."

"You better take a boatload of before and after pics."

"Of course."

"I don't think you should keep lying to Hudson, though. That's a bad idea. But you've been through the wringer, so I'll cut you some *temporary* slack."

Ronnie heard the roar of Hudson's truck before the headlights beamed through the front window. "Thank you, a thousand times, Reese! I have to run." Ronnie's heart raced as the door knob clicked. She felt like a little kid again, hiding a big secret from Hudson. Only she wasn't a kid anymore.

"Ronnie?"

"Yeah?"

"Don't work the whole time. You *are* in cowboy country."

Ronnie tucked her feet beneath her on the chair and tried not looking guilty. It was certainly too late to dash into the guest room or pretend to be asleep. To Reese, she whispered, "I'll try. Gotta go."

"Sorry that took so long," Hudson said as he entered the house. Only he didn't close the door behind him. Someone followed.

Colten.

"Mrs. Miller insisted I wait for the spinach and mushroom quiche to finishing baking." He waved a container. "She didn't want my little sister to starve in the morning while I'm out working."

Ronnie could only vaguely recall the details of the errand. Something about a loose hand railing, maybe? She wouldn't embarrass herself any further in front of Colten by asking. "How sweet of her."

"Nice pajamas." The smirk on Colten's face made her cheeks flush. "Are those chocolate moose?"

"For your information, yes. They're my favorite pajama pants." Ronnie pushed out of the chair, unrattled by this unexpected guest, triumphant in her escape of the man-swallowing recliner. The tiny cabin felt much more cramped with Colten there. "Hudson, I'm heading to bed. If you and your *guest* could keep it down, I would be grateful."

"Of course." Hudson took two strides toward her

and wrapped her in a bear hug. "It's good you're here, sis. I missed you."

"Missed you, too." In the safeguard of her brother's hug, she could pretend Colten wasn't there. He was a reminder of her mounting lies. Had he said anything about finding her at the storage lot? Ronnie would eventually muster the courage to tell Hudson about the job. Preferably when she had the best prospects of getting it back. But she didn't want to worry him about not having a place to live.

"I probably won't see you until close to dinner tomorrow." He held her at arm's length. "Will that be okay?"

"No worries." She stepped back into her bedroom to close the door, careful to avoid the curious blue eyes of the cowboy standing in the too-close background. "I'll be busy with measurements and making plans most of the day." That was, if Reese was able to snag that phone call and convince Becca she was employable.

CHAPTER 5

olten

COLTEN'S AUNT Violet was the best cook in the county, many argued, her full table at mealtimes a testament. She carried a heaping plate of buns to the center of the large table, one able to accommodate the Livingston ranch crew for meals. "I think you might give him some time off," Violet told her husband Joe.

"I can still help out some," Colten argued. "Just want to help Mom get her house ready for sale." They'd made an arrangement this week to reduce Colten's hours. He'd help move cattle, but most of the other tasks would be handled by the rest of the crew. What no one brought up was how this reduction would probably continue until Colten left for good. But the solemn expressions fixated on the tabletop seemed to imply it was on everyone's mind.

Colten had spent the better part of his morning checking the water tanks in the summer pastures, ensuring all the lines were thawed and rusted holes patched over. They'd be moving a herd at the end of the week, and those surprises were never fun to discover after a long day of driving steers five miles down the road. Most cooperated, but there were always one or two rebels in any group of cattle.

Last summer he and Hudson had spent almost four hours convincing one comfortable heifer wallowing in a muddy creek to rejoin her herd.

Sometime this week, he'd bring Hudson and his cousin Jed back to the pasture to mend the winter-damaged fence. But today he asked Uncle Joe to cut him loose early. His mom had left town after lunch, and Colten wanted to assess the damage Hudson's sister might be creating with her little project.

Colten cleaned his plate and carried it to the sink. Aunt Violet scolded him the way she did every time. She didn't like anyone in her kitchen, but he didn't want her to wait on him every second. It was a comical dance between them, started when Colten was a boy mucking out stalls. He'd miss it.

The house Colten grew up in sat a couple of miles from the ranch, down a road built over gently rolling hills. His dad had preferred the arrangement, to have his space away from the heart of the ranch. Though he and his brother had taken over when their father passed, Joe was the only one who wanted to live on the ranch.

Back at his mom's, the familiar driveway came into view near a cluster of tall trees, and Colten slowed for the turn.

Though he wasn't sure what to expect with this city designer let loose, he certainly hadn't expected to find her on the roof of the wraparound porch, stretching her cellphone toward the sky.

She didn't look his way. A loose, flowing gray sweater hid half a pair of fitted jeans. His eyes trailed down to her feet. "Heels?" he called out, slamming the truck door shut.

Ronnie squeaked, and he instantly regretted startling her. She wobbled a bit as he raced around the side of the house. She gripped a second-story windowsill and the rocking stopped. "They're wedges, thank you."

"What?"

"My shoes. They're not heels. They're *wedges*." She lifted one leg and shook the heel of the ridiculous sandal to prove her point.

"You climb people's roofs for fun or is this some super-secret designer trick to gain perspective?"

Her eyes narrowed in his direction. "Very funny."

"Did you even look for a ladder?" Colten asked,

still too stunned to process. "How'd you squirrel your way up there to begin with?" He spied the metal ladder, propped against the side of a nearby shed. When Ronnie's eyes connected with it too, her cheeks reddened.

"Your mom doesn't have Internet," she said, as if that answered everything.

"So, you thought you'd find a Wi-Fi signal up there?" Colten moved to retrieve the ladder, shaking his head in disbelief as he walked. He'd met different women before, but he'd never met one who'd crawl onto a roof for something unattainable.

"I was searching for a data signal," Ronnie supplied when he positioned the top of the ladder against the eave of the house.

"Mom probably turned off the Wi-Fi before she left."

"What?" Ronnie's hand still firmly gripped the windowsill as she squatted, reaching for the top of the ladder with her other hand. But it was too far to stretch. "Why would she do that? I need Wi-Fi to do my job."

"You're going to have to let go of that window sooner or later. Unless you expect those legs to grow a couple more feet in the next few minutes."

"Just hold the ladder," Ronnie snapped. Easing onto her knees, she crawled backward until her wedge hit the top rung.

Colten still couldn't believe she'd climbed up

there in those shoes. How a person could walk in them on a flat surface without twisting an ankle was a mystery to him. But climbing? He couldn't see it. "How'd you get up there anyway?"

"Through the window."

He followed her nod to the same window whose sill she'd been gripping. "You're supposed to leave it open, so you can climb back inside."

"Tell me something I don't know."

He held the ladder steady, eyes down, giving her room to climb, but his focus never left the wedges. Sure enough, one slipped. Colten sprang forward to catch her. Only Ronnie didn't fall. She glared at him over her shoulder. "Do you mind?"

His arms were hugging her calves. His forehead up against—

Despite an attempt to respond, Colten found his words suddenly caught in his throat. A vanilla scent engulfed his senses. It made him a little dizzy for an embarrassing moment as he backed up and her wedges thudded against the ground.

"Can you turn it back on?" Ronnie asked.

"Sure," Colten said. "But why's it so important?"

"I have to look up materials, prices, stores. Unless Starlight is hiding an array of flooring wholesalers not listed in your phonebook?"

Colten laughed, amused that she'd been resourceful enough to find a phonebook. Did people still use those? "Did you try the hardware store?

Ernie's willing to order just about anything you need."

"How fast can it be here?" Ronnie dusted off her sweater and rounded him to get to the front porch. "I don't have a lot of time. There's a lot to do."

That last statement sat uneasily with Colten. "Just what exactly does Mom have you doing?"

"Nothing drastic." Ronnie was already on the porch, reaching for the screen door. "Flooring, walls, doors, window treatments. But it's not a quick process. I can't wait for materials to show up a week from now and expect to make the deadline."

"You planning to go into Gillette?" Colten followed her to the front of the porch but didn't take the steps. "That's about your closest option. Or Cheyenne."

She'd spun away from him, her shoulders dropping. Her fingers curled around the screen door handle like she might yank it off. Colten couldn't figure out if she was irritated or about to cry. He shouldn't even care. He should let her fail so his mom could see what a waste of money this all was. He could do most of the work himself, if she'd only let him.

If only this weren't Hudson's sister.

"Why don't you come into town with me and have a look around?" He waved her toward their cars. "We can stop by and get your car fixed. You might be surprised what Starlight has to offer."

"You don't have anything better to do?" Ronnie asked, and he recognized her weak attempts to keep her walls erected.

"I need to get some paint and primer," he added. "You might as well come along."

"You painting your house?"

"No, I'm painting this one."

Panic flared in her eyes, and Colten couldn't help but laugh. "Easy there. The *outside.* Will that interfere with your design plans?"

Ronnie shook her head.

"Good. So grab your keys. Follow me to the body shop. I'll call Trent and let him know you're coming."

COLTEN HELD the door to Ernie's Hardware open for her. Ronnie's head was buried in her oversized purse, her hand lost inside to the elbow. Colten half expected a tiny, yappy puppy to emerge. But it was just a spiral notebook.

"You know about pen and paper?" he teased. "Thought all you city girls were reliant on smart-phones and tablets."

Her hair-trigger outrage was growing on him. The fire in her eyes was adorable, and he found himself trying harder to give her a reason to flash that cute little glare. Colten had known fierce women whose glares were to be feared, but Ronnie wasn't one of them.

"I like writing things down. It helps me remember them better." She fished out a marker, prepared to scratch items off a full-page list. "Plus, batteries die." She looked around the store, and Colten saw it for a moment through Ronnie's eyes, probably much smaller than what she was accustomed to. "Where are the carts?"

"I think Ernie has a couple near that far corner." Colten pointed, then led her there though she could probably find it on her own. He should talk to Ernie about paint, but something about this girl intrigued him. Ernie wasn't at the front counter anyway, so he'd use the time to find out about the storage unit.

She pulled out one of the three carts and scanned the store. "Probably easiest to go down every aisle."

Colten glanced at her list, seeing anything from wallpaper stripper to paper towels to an edging knife. "Let me see what you've got there. I have tools, if you need to borrow any."

"I was planning on it, actually." Her admission came out quiet and sheepish. "Your mom mentioned you had a circular saw. Maybe know someone with a tile cutter?"

"Tile cutter?"

"The fireplace. That old subway tile needs to go.

It dates the whole room. I'm replacing it with a more modern tile. Something gray. Maybe marble."

"But I love that tile." Colten waited for her surprised reaction before he let out a laugh. "Kidding. I'll help you bust out that old tile. I've got a sledgehammer, so you can mark that off your list. I've always hated that subway tile." His dad had too. That made him smile. Maybe she'd let him help tear that down.

Colten wasn't prepared to talk about his dad. Not with a practical stranger, no matter how alluring. The wound was too fresh and the words out of grasp anyway. "I think Mom didn't want me to get attached. I knew she'd sell soon. Just didn't expect it to be now."

"Did you grow up in that house?"

"Yeah. It belonged to my grandparents before my parents." It'd be sad to see it sold to someone outside the family, but Colten couldn't chase his dream working for Glacier National Park if he was living several hours away in Starlight.

Their gazes met, and he thought Ronnie would ask more questions he wasn't interested in answering. Instead, she returned focus to the task at hand. "Does Ernie do samples?"

"Paint samples, sure."

"Tile? Flooring? Trim?"

"You don't need new trim, there's some out in the shed. I've been ready to replace what's in the house, but my mom always makes an excuse to keep me away from projects." His mom was probably worried that if he started on the house, he'd never stop. He'd never leave Starlight.

Ronnie smirked, her eyes the color of melted chocolate meeting his. "You that horrible with tools?"

"I can handle my tools just fine, thank you."

"That remains to be seen." Ronnie was teasing. He liked this look even better than that cute glare. "Know a place around here that'll rent a dumpster?"

"Dumpster now. Going big?"

"You didn't think I was leaving that teal carpet, did you? It has to be ten years old."

"Try closer to twenty." The cute way Ronnie's eyes widened made Colten smile. "I can make a call." Though he still held suspicions about her reasons for coming to town, he wasn't about to sabotage her. Maybe his *assistance* might help him pry the truth out of her. "See if I can have one delivered this afternoon."

"Thank you."

He studied her until her she couldn't take his silence anymore. He blurted, "That might be the first time you said something nice to me."

She bumped him with her shoulder, the contact sending a charge through him. "Well, don't get used it to." Her smiled promised otherwise.

"I see Ernie," Colten lied, needing some space

before anything else confusing happened between them. “I’m going to go talk to him about paint.”

Colten knew he should keep his distance, if for no other reason than she was his best friend’s little sister. Plus, the last thing he needed was to get mixed up with another city girl. Ronnie Ross was a puzzle Colten found himself wanting to solve. The question was, why did he care? She wouldn’t stick around long enough for it to matter. And his heart couldn’t take another beating like the last.

CHAPTER 6

onnie

Becca Livingston had given Ronnie a budget and free rein. "I know the house needs a lot of updating. My only goal's to get it sold quick. Do what you feel you must, but don't go over budget. You do, that's on your dime."

In any other circumstance, Ronnie might have approached this all differently. Completed her design blueprint *before* demolition. But that worn teal carpet was scrambling her designer's brain.

It had to be the carpet, not the project's pressure.

Right before Ronnie left Hudson's cabin that morning, her phone dinged several times. Text alerts from Reese. *Ding, ding, ding* all in a row. Reese always had a lot to say and Ronnie's frayed nerves hadn't been able to take them all in. Later, she'd have to go back, read through each one more thoroughly.

Had she been back in Chicago, Ronnie'd have endless suppliers at her fingertips. Competition alone was enough to get solid discounts and free deliveries. But here in Starlight, an hour from the closest small city—if it could even be called a city—meant there'd be delivery charges to figure in. Since Ernie didn't carry any tile and his flooring options left a lot to be desired, Ronnie might have no choice but to leave town to find materials.

"The dumpster should be here in about an hour," Colten called from the kitchen doorway, shaking her from her dilemma.

"Good." Ronnie closed her laptop. It wasn't helping her make a plan anyway, she decided. "I'd like to get the carpet out today."

Colten turned his attention to the white clock over the fireplace. "Ever torn out carpet on your own before?"

No, she most definitely had not. She'd helped. Twice. But she'd watched crews do it enough to muddle her way through. "Usually there's a crew to help." That was safer than admitting she wasn't entirely sure what to do. "I'll manage."

"It's heavy. You know that, right?" Colten seemed determined to rain on her parade.

Ronnie dug through the paper sack from Ernie's

hardware, pulling out a carpet knife. "That's why I have this." At least she knew that. "I can cut it up in smaller strips. Easier hauling it out."

"If you say so."

She'd give anything to have a crew at hand to help with the demo. With the project in general. But the budget wouldn't allow any hires. It might mean she didn't get paid either, but if it helped win her job back—it'd be worth the cost.

Maybe Hudson could lend a hand if he was willing after working at the ranch. She could bribe him with her butterscotch brownies. More than once those homemade brownies had come through for her. "Might be a late night," she admitted. "But your mom told me I could stay here if I wanted."

"Did she, now?"

Ronnie'd yet to pick out a bedroom from the three guest rooms upstairs. She'd wanted to let Hudson know first, before her stuff was packed and gone. "Yep."

"Funny, because she told me I could stay, too."

Ronnie's eyes widened. "No."

Colten laughed. "Isn't really up to you, is it?"

The last thing she needed was being with Colten in the same house, even if he spent half his days at the ranch. It was bad enough how determined he was about repainting the exterior. But quite another thing for him to be sleeping here too.

Ronnie's phone dinged again, this time giving

her a much-needed excuse to get away from Colten. She stepped out onto the porch, expecting Reese, but read a text from her brother. The signal today was one bar stronger than yesterday, at least allowing text messages to come through easily enough.

Hudson: Sorry, going to be late tonight. Cow escaped. Still tracking her down.

The urge to crumple into a little ball was hard to fight. But she wouldn't break down. Not on Day One of her first solo project. She *could* do this. Somehow.

She typed a message back, telling Hudson she'd be staying at Becca's. Better to get her stuff now than to fall asleep later in her dirty clothes. She raised her hand, holding her phone high in the air to ensure the message sent, then quickly turned back inside to retrieve her keys. She collided with what might as well be a brick wall—well, something close to one anyway.

Her hands flattened against Colten's muscular chest, and she gasped. The man had to be made of steel, and Ronnie's hands, a magnet she couldn't seem to tug away. Firm hands rested on her shoulders. "Easy there."

His annoying smirk made her shoot back a couple of steps. "I need to get my suitcase."

"I'll be here." The annoying smirk remained. He faced the porch wall. "Lots of old paint to scrape."

Ronnie slipped around him, managing to avoid contact lest she burn her hands. She couldn't think about any of that now. So what if Colten stayed here too? He'd be gone to the ranch most mornings, working on the paint job during the day and sleeping the rest of the time. They could coexist. As long as he stayed outside as much as possible, they'd be fine.

RONNIE DRAGGED her heaviest suitcase up the narrow hardwood stairs. They creaked beneath her weight with each step. Colten probably thought she traveled with so much baggage simply because she lived in the city. But it was better to let him think that than admit every piece of clothing she owned was stuffed in these two suitcases. She lugged it into the room she picked and turned for the next; it too was big enough to stow a small human.

The only direction she'd been given from Becca was to leave the bedroom at the south end of the hall alone as it was hers. Though she was prepared to sell, she'd not gotten to packing up anything in there yet, unlike the rest of the house. Most of the furniture downstairs was gone, and what was left they'd stuffed into an office to be moved out of the way for renovations.

Opening each door in this hallway one at a time, Ronnie discovered a linen closet lined with sparse floor-to-ceiling shelves, a roomy bathroom with a much too small vanity counter, and three additional bedrooms.

It was the last room on the left that grabbed her. Though Ronnie would've painted the mint green walls a soft gray—and might if time and budget allowed—the fluffy white comforter with its light blue throw pillows called to her.

Ronnie tucked her second suitcase into a wide closet and headed back downstairs. There was still so much to do.

Colten seemed to be making good time with his scraping. The side without the wraparound porch was already done, his blue ground tarp covered in paint flakes. Maybe she should tell him which bedroom she picked, to ensure he wouldn't try stealing it back.

Ronnie rounded the corner to the back of the house and froze. Colten, leaning against the ladder with headphones in, was furiously at work with the scraper, sweat dripping down the back of his neck . . . and missing his shirt. Ronnie swallowed and high-tailed it away before he caught her staring.

Why was her heart beating so erratically at the sight of a man without his shirt? It wasn't as if she'd never seen that before. In fact, Ronnie saw it all the time when the cameras were done filming for the day. Many of her projects were spent in the summer without air conditioning.

She cast her mind back to that one time when duct work was being moved, how the crew had stripped it off in the Chicago humidity. But she'd never been affected quite like this. "Carpet. I need to start on the carpet."

To her dismay, the dumpster still hadn't shown up. The lowered sun suggested it might be tomorrow before one arrived. But that didn't mean she couldn't start. She could leave the carpet rolls on the porch. Toss them in tomorrow.

With the Wi-Fi now functioning and Ronnie's stomach rumbling, she brought her laptop into the kitchen to pull up online videos of how to tear out carpet while she fixed herself a ham and cheese sandwich from the leftovers Becca insisted she eat.

"How to Rip Up Old Grungy Carpet," Ronnie read aloud from her YouTube choice. "Bingo!"

The video seemed easy enough to follow. Ronnie jotted down the tools she'd need: mini crowbar, hammer, floor scraper. *Would Ernie have one in stock?* The short clip made her confidence soar. Ripping out carpet should be a breeze! Sure, pulling up the tack strips would take some muscle and time, but she could do this.

Finishing her sandwich, she rinsed off her plate in the sink, thinking how Becca'd mentioned some tools in the shed out back. The rest Ronnie hoped Colten could bring over tomorrow. He was too focused, *and* much too shirtless, for her to bother him now.

THE SMALL SHED door creaked when she opened it. Sunlight illuminated the heavy layer of dust and streams of cobwebs. Cobwebs meant spiders. Ronnie took a deep breath. No one was going to dig through these tools for her. Maybe if she went back to the house and got a broom to knock down the cobwebs she wouldn't hyperventilate.

"Need something?"

She jumped and let loose a startled scream. "Colten! You don't sneak up on a girl when spiders are involved."

"You city girls don't have spiders?" That annoying smirk was back. At least he had the decency to put his shirt back on, or she'd be a stammering idiot right now.

"Of course we have spiders. Doesn't mean I have to like them."

"What are you looking for?"

Her eyes scanned the shed, hoping to find her prize before Colten could come to her rescue. Before the dust tickling her nose caused a sneezing fit was also a consideration. But nothing in here resembled what she needed. "A small crowbar? For the tacks."

"Got one in my truck."

Ronnie evaluated him then, but instantly

regretted it. His blue eyes were too blue. Too intense up close like this. "You just happen to drive around with a carpet crowbar in your truck?"

"Comes in handy for fixing fence out on the ranch." He stepped back, allowing her to free herself from the cobwebs. "C'mon, I'll get it. You won't find anything useful in that shed unless you're looking for a pet with eight or more legs."

She skittered away from the spider-infested shed and followed him to his truck, waiting as he climbed into the bed. After some shuffling in the aluminum toolbox, he pulled out just the tool she had in mind. "This work?"

"Yep."

"Need anything else?"

She needed help, but no way she'd ask for it. "Nope. Unless you have a floor scraper in there."

He just laughed and dug some more. "Here." Handing her a pair of needle-nose pliers, he advised, "You'll need this."

"Oh." Ronnie just stared at the small tool for a moment, dread coursing through her at the thought of pulling each and every staple out by hand. But she wasn't about to give Colten Livingston one more reason to smirk at her dilemma. She reached for the pliers, ignoring the graze of his skin, and the unwanted tingles that touch caused.

Eager to be free of Colten, she hurried into the house. After shoving the lone recliner into the office with everything else, she carried out a small side table. Ronnie surveyed the empty living room. Just as the video instructed, she picked out a corner to begin her demo.

"You can do this, Ronnie," she mumbled to herself and squatted down. She wedged the crowbar under the edge of the carpet and yanked. Nothing happened. Pulling back, she shoved the crowbar down a little farther, hoping she'd get the edge under the carpet. Ronnie pulled again. When nothing budged, she pulled harder.

The crowbar slipped.

And of course, Ronnie went flying backwards, landing on her bottom with a hard thud. She groaned. "Stupid crowbar." She checked over her shoulder to ensure Colten hadn't been nearby, observing her pathetic skills.

Reassured, she tried again. This time, the corner pulled up, just like in the video. She continued to pull it back, finding this part fairly easy. But the blue padding she expected to be underneath wasn't there. The ancient pad she did reveal was a discolored yellow. And chunks of it disintegrated into dust before her eyes.

The video hadn't explained how to remove carpet spanning a twenty-foot-long room. So after gauging what she could carry out to the porch on her own, Ronnie took to the knife and began cutting. Sometimes the blade went through the carpet like butter. Then it would hit a snag, for no reason she could see, and it forced her to use her muscles.

By the time dusk settled in, her shirt was soaked through in places, sticking to her dusty, itchy skin. She was exhausted. Only one strip was fully out, leaving two thirds of the room still untouched. Yellow carpet pad dust hung everywhere, and the number of staples still in the floor was more than she could count. The video made that part look so easy. But unless Ernie had a floor scraper, she'd still be pulling up staples next spring.

Her muscles ached, her nose felt clogged, and she was filthy. All Ronnie wanted tonight was a hot shower and a comfortable bed. Tomorrow, she'd get up early and start again. Maybe it would be easier when the dumpster arrived and she could actually throw things away. If some of the unneeded clutter was cleared out, she'd feel like more was accomplished.

Colten was still outside, scraping away. She'd managed to avoid him most of the day, which was for the best. He had some sort of spotlight turned onto the side of the house. As long as it didn't come in through her bedroom window, Ronnie didn't care. If they could steer clear of each other, it'd be easier to forget him sleeping under the same roof.

After a shower, Ronnie crawled under the covers in her chocolate moose pajama pants and was asleep moments after she turned out the light.

CHAPTER 7

olten

IT HAD TAKEN all afternoon and late into the evening, but every last piece of the clapboard siding was free from its old layer of paint. Though too dark to see the progress in the whole, Colten imagined the house looked gray now without its chipped light blue color.

Colten's muscles ached, and blisters lined his already-rough hands. Though he promised his cousin they'd go fishing on their mutual day off, he hoped Jed would be willing to put in some time layering on primer. Ernie knew a guy who'd be willing to lend him a sprayer for a couple of days in exchange for some fence repair work.

After a hot shower, he sluggishly made his way down the dark hallway, too weary even to flip on the overhead light. His old room had become his dad's bedroom toward the end—where he could rest in solitude and comfort and sleep throughout the day as he desired. Colten couldn't bring himself to open the door, much less sleep in there.

He assumed Ronnie had taken the bedroom on the right. It was full of purple flowers and other girly stuff his grandma had preferred for her visits. Visits that wouldn't happen any longer since Becca had decided on moving back to Denver where Grandma Rose lived.

In the dimness, Colten opened the last door on the left and slipped inside. He'd noticed how far the carpet removal hadn't progressed downstairs. But he didn't want to disturb Ronnie by slamming any doors. He closed it as quietly as he could. Her day had probably been just as labor intensive as his.

In only his pajama bottoms, Colten crawled beneath his covers and fell almost instantly into deep sleep.

THE FIRST TRACES of sunlight peeked through the windows, stabbing Colten's eyes. He blinked awake, still in an exhausted daze. Something warm weighed down his chest. It took him a moment to focus. A tangle of dark brown hair and the scent of vanilla shampoo infiltrated his senses.

In his tired stupor, Colten hadn't thought to turn on a light last night. Otherwise he'd have seen Ronnie already in his room.

And now, asleep on his chest, her arm curled around him like a cocoon, all he could focus on was his hand snaked around her back. How had this happened? If either of them had figured it out in the middle of the night, there would've been screaming. Or yelling. So much yelling.

If he just peeled himself away, maybe they didn't need to talk about this. Only he would know. And he'd certainly not make the mistake of crawling in with her again. He hesitated, wondering how best to move without waking her.

Or maybe he hesitated because of the way she felt in his arms. Like she belonged there. Colten brushed away that thought. Not only was she not staying, she was Hudson's little sister. That thought made his panic rise. What if she did wake up and discover their entanglement? Would she run, tell Hudson instead of listening about a genuine misunderstanding? No matter how one looked at this situation, no matter how innocent, it looked bad.

With one hand, he combed back her hair, tucking the soft strands behind her ear. He didn't want any to get tangled when he slid out. Her waking up screaming in pain surely would cause more problems than they needed. It was then that he noticed streaks on her cheeks. They stretched from her eyes to her jawline.

Tears?

In what could only be considered a series of perfect ninja moves, he successfully slithered out without waking her. Ronnie snuggled into a pillow when they broke contact, and already he felt emptier without her touch. But he pushed the thought away and hurried out of the room, his heart pounding as he padded softly down the hallway. She seemed so put together, so confident. What could she possibly have to cry over?

COLTEN BLAZED the two miles down the gravel road to the Livingston ranch to pick up his fifteen-year-old cousin Jed. He'd ruin the kid's day. There wasn't much downtime working for Jed's dad, Joe. He gave everyone one day off, and it just so happened that Jed and Colten had today off.

Jed sat perched on his front porch, two fishing rods in hand, a tackle box beside him. Lou's eyes were bright and her bushy tail wagged at dangerous speeds when she spotted the truck. Colten usually let her spend Thursday evenings with Jed. Even the dog would be disappointed when she learned fishing was no longer on the agenda.

"Sorry," Colten called over when he hopped out of the truck. "I need a favor."

"So, no fishing? I was hoping to bring home supper tonight."

Colten couldn't resist those disappointed eyes. It was as if the kid was still eight, the way that look was breaking Colten's heart. "This is a paying favor." Colten hoped the bribery would work. "But go ahead and bring your rod. We'll try to squeeze in some time later today."

Jed lit up, his smile returning, and tossed his fishing poles in the back of the truck. Lou ran a couple of circles around the truck, waiting for the tailgate to drop. "What's the job?"

The words surprised Colten. "Ever ripped up carpet?"

Jed shook his head. "Nope."

He'd planned to have Jed help him with the priming today. Maybe waking up with Ronnie in his arms made him feel sympathy for her impossible situation. Or the tear streaks did it.

She put up a tough exterior, but underneath that thick layer, the girl was hiding something. He'd suspected that from the moment he met her at the storage units, but only now did he realize that a secret burdened her, whatever it was. Maybe it even made her afraid.

"Well, today you get to learn." At the pitiful look on the kid's face, Colten couldn't help but laugh.

"I'm buying lunch. So, at least you've got that going."

When they swung by Colten's house, he made a quick call while he let Jed dig out his shop vacuum and lug it to the truck. "Chuck, that dumpster was supposed to be there yesterday," he said into the phone. "What's the hangup?" After some back and forth, Colten finally relented. "Your next meal at the Starlight Bar and Grill's on me. Whatever you want. Just get that dumpster out there this morning. We'll have it filled by this afternoon."

Colten retrieved two other toolboxes from his garage, a circular saw, and a new bag of shop rags. Back on the road, he headed into town. He swung by the hardware store and found a gently used floor scraper on sale—the only one Ernie had in stock.

On the way to the house, Jed asked, "Who you think's going to buy Aunt Becca's house?"

"Not sure."

"What about you?"

Colten turned to look at Jed then. "Me?"

"Yeah. Why not? Lots of land. That barn, you could put a couple horses like you talked about once." Jed fiddled with his phone for a moment, then stuck it back in his pocket. "Unless you're leaving too?"

"I'm not looking to buy a house just yet." It felt like the safest answer he could give. The news that his mom was selling caught him off guard only because who'd expected it so soon? She was right, though. It might be time to start making some calls. But until something was lined up, Colten wouldn't concern Jed.

"But you'll need your own someday."

"Someday." Colten wasn't sure that was true. At one time, he dreamt of inheriting the family home. He pictured raising a family there with someone he loved. Sitting on the front porch in rocking chairs and sipping on a beer, watching the stars. But Danica killed that dream when she hightailed it out of town two years ago. Crumpled his heart in the dust trail.

"What if where you move doesn't let you have horses?" Jed pointed out.

"I can keep them at the ranch," Colten countered. But he knew that wasn't the same thing. He'd wanted a place with a barn since he was a little boy. But horses would have to wait until he knew what his future held.

"You could pay me to take care of them," Jed offered quickly. "I need to save up for a truck anyway."

"Well, ripping out carpet will help you with that."

Colten's first thought was that this kid needed to stop growing. The thought that Jed would be driving in just a few months was a scary representation of how quickly time was passing. The last two years since Danica left had disappeared in a quick, tumultuous blur.

Catching sight of Lou in his rearview mirror, her mouth open, tail wagging, Colten smiled. If it hadn't been for Lou, he wasn't sure what his life would've become.

Lou jumped out the second the tailgate was down. An Australian shepherd needed more exercise than Lou was getting on a regular basis. One day a week to run free while they fished wasn't cutting it. But Colten couldn't take her out to run around the ranch outside of the small cluster of cabins and the main house. Lou was still very skittish around the cattle, and he suspected she always would be.

"Let's get all this stuff to the porch. I need to check with Ronnie and see where she wants us to start." Colten didn't want to admit his nervousness, seeing her. Would she have any recollection that they'd somehow wound up in each other's arms last night?

If he stayed focused on the task at hand, maybe he wouldn't think about it. He'd helped tear out carpet once before. Old, old carpet. If this teal carpet was anything like that, they only wanted to move it once.

He didn't see Ronnie immediately, but he heard the clicking of her camera phone. She had to be in the kitchen. He thought to interrupt her and ask where she wanted everything, but one look at her and he froze with his mouth halfway open. She'd rolled up the sleeves of her loose, light sweater, and her long, wavy hair was pulled back in a bun twisted on the top of her head. The same hair that'd been spread across his chest just a couple of hours ago.

"Before and after pictures," Ronnie said, sensing his presence but not turning from her clicking.

"For?" It wasn't as if his mom would care. She just wanted the house in good enough shape to sell.

"Portfolio." She snapped a few more, then set her phone on the table. It was then he spotted those crazy wedged sandals.

"You own any other shoes?"

"I like my shoes." Reaching for a clipboard, she faced him. He caught a smudge of dirt on her right cheekbone. Colten felt annoyed for thinking she looked almost cute in that moment.

"You're checking up on me, right? I just stopped to jot down a few notes about the kitchen." She tapped at the lined paper. Made a sharp tic mark. "I'll get back to work."

Before he could answer, the beeping of equipment backing up interrupted. "Your dumpster's here." He nodded toward the front door. "I'll have them put it right off the porch."

Ronnie nodded. "Good thinking. Grass isn't really nice enough to worry about killing. You might be doing the lawn a favor, actually."

The cuteness evaporated. "I hope you're not

planning to waste any of that budget on sod. Folks around here don't care if their grass is perfect and green. We like it with a little mix of color. Especially on the far edges of town."

"And weeds?" Ronnie challenged.

"Wildflowers." Colten took *that* as his cue to leave. Even if she didn't know it, they'd be stuck together the rest of the day. Being at odds over a lawn seemed a little stupid. As soon as the dumpster was set, he and Jed would rip out the rest of the carpet. And he'd be done with it.

Colten made it outside as Chuck's truck drove away. Jed had read his mind, which was a good thing considering they weren't manhandling the dumpster to any other spot. All the tools and supplies got unloaded, and Lou sat guard by them on the porch. But her darting eyes said she itched to run.

"Go on, Lou. Take a lap."

The pup sprang to her feet and leapt off the porch. She circled the house in a sprint, her tail wagging furiously.

"See, Lou loves it here," Jed prodded.

"Who's Lou?"

Ronnie'd snuck up on them both. Colten saw Jed started a little at her unexpected appearance. His fault for leaving the front door wide open.

"Lou's the dog, ma'am."

Ronnie's eyes lit up at the sight of Lou, something that caught Colten off guard. When the two made eye contact, Lou cut her third circle short and charged toward the house, right up the stairs to Ronnie.

Ronnie knelt in greeting, rubbing Lou with both hands. "Hi, Lou! Aren't you a beautiful dog!" Lou soaked up every second. When she licked Ronnie's cheek, Ronnie actually laughed and gave her a hug.

Colten was taken aback by this. Danica had hated dogs. He thought most city girls did, unless they could fit them in their purse like little barking trophies. But Ronnie seemed right at home with Lou, as if they were old pals.

"She's a beautiful dog. Australian shepherd?" she asked upon standing. Lou, done with her squiggling, jetted down the steps to get in another lap.

"Yeah." Words seemed to fail Colten now. "You have a dog? Back home?"

The light in Ronnie's eyes dimmed. She dipped her head, shaking it. "No. I'm never at home enough."

"I've never ripped up carpet before," Jed said, an oddly excited light in his eyes.

"You . . ." Confusion lingered in her expression as she looked between Jed and Colten. "You've come to rip up carpet?"

"Colten said we were."

"Unless you don't want the help?" Colten tried sounding cool, collected. But meeting her puzzled gaze, his voice trembled a bit. He couldn't wash away the feeling of her curled up against his chest. Helping her was maybe the worst idea he'd had yet. And Colten had plenty of bad ideas lately. But the memory of those tear-streaked cheeks won out.

"I thought you were painting."

"I have time. Mom won't be back for a few days." Spotting the floor scraper propped up against the stairs, Colten went to grab it. "Found you a present."

The happiness that spread over Ronnie's face made him burst with pride, though he couldn't explain why. It was only a floor scraper. One that'd save her lots of back-breaking labor. Better than stooping over with a pair of needle-nose pliers all day. But nothing more than that.

"You boys just earned yourself some butterscotch brownies." Turning to go back inside, she added over her shoulder, "Who's ready to rip up some carpet?"

CHAPTER 8

onnie

At the first bite of her bacon cheeseburger, Ronnie realized how ravenous she was. Her eyes closed as she relished the amazing flavor. The toasted bun, perfectly cooked burger, the crunch of bacon, crisp along the edges. She was in heaven.

"Glad you took a break?" Jed asked. The kid was sweet, and a hard worker from what she'd seen. She wasn't sure what she would have done if they hadn't helped get all the carpet out today.

"I'm not always so great about remembering to eat." She avoided Colten's inquisitive glance and pushed her sleeves back up. Ronnie'd been a hot sweaty mess when they left the house for a bite to eat in town. At least now her light sweater wasn't pasted on her like fly paper.

It was a shame Jed worked so many hours at the ranch. Between bites he promised, "I could come back and help if you want. My next day off. If I can. Ma'am." Colten only offered a small head shake to that, so Ronnie didn't expect to see much more of Jed before her time was up.

"How can you forget to eat?" Jed's next question seemed genuine, his eyebrows drawn in curiosity as his burger hovered over his plate, clamped in both hands. Whatever he ordered had twice as much food between the buns as her cheeseburger.

"When you work nonstop to meet a deadline, it happens."

"We've worked sixteen-hour days branding cattle," Jed continued. "Never forgot I was hungry."

Colten laughed quietly, his shoulders shaking. Lou whined beneath the table, her eyes darting between raised hands.

"Guess I get wrapped up in the work." She shrugged, no longer sure how to describe her reality. Or what used to be her reality. There might be plenty of time to remember meals if she didn't convince Lana to give her the job back. "I'll make those brownies I promised soon. Colten's responsible for seeing you get your fair share."

"I'm not responsible if something happens during transit," Colten interjected.

"You mean if you happen to eat them." This easy banter from him was new to her. They'd been spitting fire at each other since they met, then something changed. Something Ronnie couldn't pinpoint. But whatever, he had offered to help with the carpet. Ronnie had felt certain he'd let her fall flat on her face with this project. And without his help, that's exactly what would have happened.

"What's it like?" Jed asked.

Ronnie set her half-eaten burger back on her plate. "What's what like?"

"Being on TV."

Both Jed and Colten were staring now, waiting for her answer. "I wasn't on much. More of a background person."

Lana always had the spotlight. Maybe they captured a bit of witty dialogue here and there, but when they did, Ronnie had to say it twenty times until they captured a take they liked.

"Is it weird having cameras around all the time?"

Ronnie swallowed the bite she snuck in. "You get used to it. But you learn to watch what you say." Dread washed over her anew at the thought of those cameras capturing her life's most humiliating moment. They'd been known to turn around a show in less than three weeks for good ratings. What if they decided to air that before she left Starlight? Seemed half the town watched the show.

Colten finished his burger and hailed the waitress for the check. Before Ronnie could argue, he cut her off. "I told you both, dinner's on me."

"But—"

"Try, *thank you.*"

Ronnie bit back the urge to snap. If anything, she should be buying them dinner. They ripped out all the carpet in the living room, dining room, and the upstairs hallway. "Thank you." She had manners. But he probably thought she was some stuck-up city girl. One who didn't know how to use them. "And thank you both for helping me today. I'm sure you had better things to do."

She'd been hoping to find hardwood floors underneath the living room carpet, but it'd been a bitter disappointment. She'd focus on the flooring dilemma tomorrow, after some rest. There were plenty other to-do items to work on once they drove back.

"Happy to help, ma'am," Jed spoke up. Lou even barked a comment from beneath their table, but her gaze was intently fixed on a fry in Colten's hand. "I mean, we were going to go fishing, but I don't mind. We can go another time, right Colten?"

"Sure," Colten agreed. "But there're still a couple of hours of daylight left. Plus, poles're already in the truck."

Guilt crept in, but how could Ronnie have known she'd impinged on plans? They hadn't mentioned them until now.

Jed lit up like a new bulb, his excitement cautious. "I bet your fishing gear's ready. We could just hit the stream by Aunt Becca's place."

"You should do that," Ronnie encouraged. It'd make her feel less guilty, and it would offer her some distance from Colten. She appreciated the help, but there'd been too much time spent watching those strong biceps at work tearing out carpet. It was muddling her brain.

"You're coming, too, aren't you?" Jed asked.

"I bet Ronnie here doesn't really care to fish. She is from *Chicago*."

Ronnie narrowed her eyes at that. "You say that like it's contagious." She turned her attention to Jed. "Thank you for the invitation, but I need to get all those staples up tonight. Then I have some paint samples to try out in the living room." The dining room walls were covered in lilac wallpaper, a task she didn't want to think about dealing with.

"Hudson wasn't kidding about you being a workaholic," Colten stated.

"Runs in the family," Ronnie replied. Hudson had once again apologized for dodging his vacation host duties. He'd been asked to stay at the ranch to help the owner build a new tool shed. "But I don't have a pole anyway."

"Sounds like an excuse to me," Colten said, his blue eyes staring in challenge.

"You can borrow my spare," Jed jumped in. "I brought two."

"Well, there you go," Colten added. "How can you back out now?"

"But—"

"The work isn't going anywhere. Besides, Jed gave up a whole day of fishing to help. Least you can do is come with us."

Ronnie should really stay behind. She'd never run an entire project on her own, much less planned and executed the whole thing. But it felt hard enough to say no to one insistent cowboy, let alone two.

The dog lifted her paw toward Ronnie, as if extending her own invitation. Ronnie scratched her behind the ears. "Well, Lou, let's go fishing."

RONNIE'S DAD spent all his free time golfing and watching college baseball. He wasn't much for the wild outdoors, and as a result, she didn't know the first thing about fishing. But she'd seen videos here and there on Facebook. How hard could it be?

"This is a really long fishing pole." Ronnie stood it next to her and found the pole towered at least six inches above her head.

"Longer pole means you can cast farther," Jed said.

"We'll be fishing from shore," Colten explained.

"Oh." Ronnie made her way back to the truck, but Colten, Jed, and even Lou raced toward the tree line behind the house. She followed them, spotting the opening in the trees as she rounded the shed.

"There's a great stream a little ways down this path," Jed told her over his shoulder. "It's deep, so brown trout love it."

Ronnie had quickly traded out her wedges for flats before following the guys down the tree-covered trail. The hard-packed dirt path was littered with tree roots and rocks the size of her head. She'd surely have twisted an ankle in those other shoes. Almost out of breath by the time they made it to the clearing, she still managed to keep up with them. But Jed had been racing Lou half the way there.

"*This* is a stream?" The water that spanned at least forty feet in width looked much more like a river.

"It's a small detour off the main river," Colten said. "Good place for fish to hide, though."

The shore, a mixture of dirt, rock, and boulders, stretched as far as Ronnie could see before it angled around groupings of trees and disappeared around another bend. "Where's the dock?"

Colten laughed. "You're looking at it."

"But . . . it's . . . that's just a big rock."

"Flat enough though, right?"

Ronnie eyed the smooth boulder with suspicion.

Considering she had no clue what to do, she wondered how long it would take for her to slip into the stream. At least she could see the bottom close to the boulder.

She kicked off her shoes and stepped onto the surface of the rock, wondering how far out one had to go to find the deep water Jed mentioned.

Jed had positioned himself on his own boulder a little farther down, casting his rod with a weird sort of sideways tossing motion. The only kind of fishing Ronnie'd ever seen involved placing the fishing pole behind and tossing it forward in an overhead arc.

"You're in luck that Jed already set you up with your lure. Now we just have to work on your casting."

Ronnie started to do what she'd seen on the one or two fishing videos, but Colten was quickly at her side, holding her arm hostage. "You're going to catch a person, not a fish with that cast." He wobbled a bit on the larger but unsteady rocks where he stood. "Here, let me help." Placing his feet on the back of her boulder didn't leave much space between them.

Tingles raced up her arms as his fingers wrapped around her wrist and his other hand rested on her arm. Afraid trying to speak might cause something alien-like to come out instead of words, she just nodded, keeping her eyes on the rod.

"We're going to practice this a couple of times," Colten warned, his words now spoken in a low tone against her ear. With his hand guiding the motion, showing her to cast the same way Jed was just down the river, he kept up the low murmur. Briefly Ronnie wondered what Jed must think of them here on this rock.

Would he say something to Hudson, give him the wrong idea? Because if someone walked up on them now, surely *they'd* get the wrong idea. No way Colten was having the same reaction to their touch. Not with how calm he seemed.

The third attempt was her best, and Colten encouraged her to leave her lure in for a few minutes. "You're doing great," he said as he hopped off her boulder and practically ran to shore for his own pole.

The air around her seemed chillier now without Colten so near. More than that, Ronnie couldn't shake this feeling of familiarity. It was ridiculous. She'd only met Colten two days ago. Hudson had mentioned a friend in past phone conversations, but not even a name had stuck from any of those calls.

Ronnie decided it was simply her lack of dating for so long that had her head scrambled. It'd been over two years since she entertained more than a couple of first dates. None ever resulted in second ones. She'd buried herself in her work, determined to realize her dreams. And that line of thinking left little time for relationships.

If Colten hadn't guilted her into fishing tonight, she'd be working right now.

He stood a few feet away, on his own boulder, casting his line with casual grace. "Don't know if we'll get any bites tonight. Might have gotten out here too late."

Ronnie secretly hoped she wouldn't catch anything for fear a fish would yank Jed's pole from her hands and send it downstream. Maybe her with it. "You go fishing a lot?"

Colten shrugged. "A bit, yeah. Jed loves it."

The insatiable need to know more about this mysterious cowboy was starting to take over, and she couldn't help the question that came next. "You lived here all your life?"

"No," Colten answered, a single, final-sounding word.

Something about asking that had shut him down, so Ronnie decided to leave it alone for now.

"You like working for Lana Bojanski?"

That caught her off guard and Ronnie almost slipped into the stream. She gained her footing at the last second, happy she left her shoes farther up on the shore. Her bare feet had better grip than flats. More traction. "*You* watch the show?"

"I've seen an episode or two." He readjusted his line. "You didn't answer my question."

Ronnie was still off-kilter with the new bit of information, but she managed a strangled reply. "Sure, I do."

"Really?" Colten asked. "I always thought she

came off as kind of ruthless, a person only out for herself."

The description, Ronnie had to admit, did seem to fit Lana to a tee. But she wouldn't admit that to Colten. Or to anyone, considering she wanted her job back more than anything. "Well, she can be—"

"Got a bite," Jed said, his voice just loud enough to carry to them. But the glow in his eyes was near blinding.

Colten hopped from his boulder to see, without even a glance at Ronnie. Seemed his impression about Lana wouldn't be easily deterred. It left Ronnie puzzling how he'd picked up on her boss's personality flaw. The producers had been careful to showcase Lana's positive traits. If that weren't the case, why would anyone watch the show?

CHAPTER 9

olten

COLTEN FIXED himself a turkey sandwich and scarfed it down in about three bites. Not a typical breakfast, just the quickest thing to get him out of the house before Ronnie got up. He'd been smart enough to sleep in a separate room last night, but it left him feeling a little empty.

None of it made any sense.

Today, he wanted to busy himself with layering the clapboard in primer. Hudson would be along any minute to help. If they finished that project, the front porch and deck both needed a good power wash and stain. A full day of working on the exterior was exactly what Colten needed to keep his mind from drifting to Ronnie and how she looked when she panicked and thought a fish had caught her line.

"A shoe? I caught a stupid shoe?" Her cute, disappointed expression had stayed with him in his dreams.

A knock on the kitchen door shook him from his thoughts, and moments later Hudson emerged. He filled the entire door frame with his broad linebacker shoulders and his need to duck to avoid the top of the frame. Colten considered himself tall at his six-two, but Hudson always made him feel small.

"Hey, man." Hudson set a box down on the table, and immediately went to scratch Lou behind the ears the way she liked. "Brought some things for Ronnie."

"Still asleep." Colten pointed a digit to the ceiling as he carried his plate to the sink.

Hudson rounded the table, poking his head into the living room. "She got a lot done yesterday."

"Not gonna miss that carpet, that's for sure."

"The paint sprayer's in my truck. Don needs it back by Tuesday."

"Thanks." Colten gulped down a glass of water. He was probably the only rancher he knew who didn't drink coffee on a regular basis. He hated the bitter flavor. "Want a sandwich?"

"Already ate. Your aunt made waffles."

Colten swiped a pair of gloves from the counter and eyed the back door. "I always miss the good meals." Colten and Hudson lived in cabins on the

Livingston ranch property. Aunt Violet always made enormous breakfasts for the crew, but you had to be early or there'd be nothing left.

"Becca know you're painting the house?"

"Nope." Colten could see his mom's sour expression now when she returned from Denver and found her weathered light blue house transformed a pale yellow with white trim and porch columns. "She doesn't even know we're staining the porch. But if she wants it sold . . ." Colten let his words trail. The thought of a stranger living in his childhood home didn't sit right. But as an only child, there wasn't anyone else unless one of his cousins wanted it.

The two headed outside. Hudson unloaded the paint sprayer while Colten got to work covering the windows with plastic and taping everything down. "Thanks for helping Ronnie out yesterday," Hudson said. "I would've been here myself, but Joe really wanted that shed up. It was the only way to convince him to let me have today off."

"Sure. Gave Jed a chance to get his hands dirty." Colten didn't want to talk about Ronnie but feared the inevitable, so he added, "We took her fishing afterward."

"My little sister? Fishing?" Hudson shook his head, laughing now. "I can't see it. Did you make her bait her own hook?"

"Nah, Jed had a lure already tied. She did catch a shoe, though."

Hudson laughed louder, but not loud enough to muffle the creaking of approaching footsteps.

"What's so funny out here?" Ronnie had come out onto the porch, hands folded around a ceramic mug. The gentle breeze carried the vanilla scent of her freshly shampooed hair and Colten found himself choked for words. In her black shorts and fitted T-shirt, she made his pulse crazy.

"I heard you had a great catch last night!" Hudson teased.

Ronnie's cheeks instantly blazed red. "It was a very *big* shoe."

"Did he have to pay you?" Hudson teased. "I didn't think I'd ever see the day my city-girl sister picked up a fishing pole."

Colten almost felt bad as her embarrassment stayed on those cheeks. "She actually picked up casting pretty quick." Admittedly, he'd been a bit disappointed at how smoothly she cast her line by her third try. Then he wished he hadn't said anything. How would Hudson feel, knowing that the two of them had stood so close together? Worse, how would his best friend feel if he found out about Colten's bedroom mix-up?

"See!" Ronnie chimed in. "Just because our parents wouldn't step foot in the outdoors without an air-conditioned motorhome doesn't mean all my genes are hopeless. You're proof of that." Ronnie stuck her tongue out at Hudson.

"You out here to help?" Hudson pointed the sprayer at the siding.

"Sorry, boys. I have staples to scrape up and tack strips to tackle." She sent a small smile Colten's way. A thank you, he thought, for the floor scraper he'd acquired. "I'll let you both get to work."

Colten fought the urge to watch her walk back indoors. "Uncle Joe been complaining any that I'm not around to help much this week?"

"Nope. He understands what you're doing."

"You mean Aunt Violet made him understand?"

Hudson chuckled. "Yeah. We'll be short with Malcom out. Steers to move tomorrow. You able to make it?"

"Yeah, I'll be there." Any excuse to avoid Ronnie seemed like a good one right now. Colten propped the ladder beside a window and started to climb. "Hand me that tape roll, would ya?"

RONNIE

Ronnie couldn't get inside fast enough. Last night she dreamt about falling asleep in Colten's arms; maybe that was making her dizzy. *And* unfocused on the main project at hand. Finishing her coffee, she rinsed her cup in the sink, then found the crowbar. She spent an hour prying up the remaining tack strips and felt proud when she sat back on her knees and sighed. "Tacks finished. Next, staples."

She'd done one thing on her own, at least.

In the kitchen to grab a drink of water, Ronnie's phone dinged, another text.

With a yawn, she considered ignoring it. She still had the wallpaper-removal project in the dining room, after all those staples to tackle. But the continued dinging got to her. What if it was Lana, desperate to have her back? She rarely had a signal strong enough to receive messages without climbing on the roof.

Mom: You're in Montana?!
Mom: Is your brother ok?!?!
Mom: Are you ok?!?!
Mom: You haven't called me all week.
Mom: Are you alive?!?!?!?!

To stop the influx of abused punctuation, Ronnie dialed back while she miraculously had three bars. Marian Ross picked up on the first ring. "I haven't heard from you in days, Veronica! You didn't tell anyone you left town!"

"Hi, Mom. I'm fine."

Leaning back against the counter, sipping on her water, she let her mom continue her worried rant for a few moments more. She'd learned the hard way that if she didn't give her the chance to unload her several unnecessary worries, she wouldn't listen to a thing Ronnie said.

"You good now?" Ronnie tried to keep the teasing edge out of her voice, but her mom seemed to hear it anyway.

"Young lady, this isn't funny. You took off to the middle of nowhere, Montana."

"Wyoming."

"I thought Hudson lived in Montana."

"Nope, it's always been Wyoming. You send him birthday and Christmas cards. Care packages!"

"My computer saves his address. And I get the two mixed up. It's one of those ranch states filled with cowboys." A worried gasp sounded from the other end. "You haven't run off to elope with some cowboy, have you?"

"Mom!" Ronnie cut in. "I'm visiting Hudson. Taking some time off."

"Veronica, you've never taken a vacation."

"Well . . ." Afraid her mom would see through her lie, she brightened her tone. "It was overdue. So, here I am."

"And didn't think to tell anyone you were leaving? How long will you be gone? When are you coming back? I didn't think you were allowed to take time off during filming."

If she were still employed, then her mom would be correct.

"Sorry, it was kind of a whim. Hudson's been

trying to talk me into visiting him for a while. So I took two weeks off."

"Honey." Marian's voice softened. "You know you could've come to stay with me and your dad. We always have the room. Taking off to Montana—"

"Wyoming."

"Yes, Wyoming. Taking off to such a remote place alone . . . that's foolish. What if something happened to you?"

"Mom, I'm twenty-six. I'm not a kid anymore." Ronnie was tired of the argument that seemed to repeat itself. Hudson, only three years older, could do whatever he wanted and be treated like an adult. But the second Ronnie did something even remotely spontaneous, Mom talked to her like a child. Before that could continue, Ronnie added, "I actually found myself a job."

"You're staying?" Panic crackled through the phone.

"No, no," Ronnie answered quickly. Though a small part of her was having a hard time imagining leaving, she chocked it up to escapist syndrome. Sure, the little Wyoming town was almost charming now. But in a week or two, reality would come crashing back and remind her that she'd been hiding from her problems. "There's a house that needs some renovations before it goes on the market. I'm overseeing the project." Ronnie didn't think it important to mention that *she* was manager and crew, basically doing all the labor, minus some part-time family help. No need to give Mom more to worry about.

"Well, that's nice then. But honey, that's hardly a vacation."

"So, it's my first one. I'm still adjusting."

"You sure you're okay?" Marian asked. "I can fly out there."

The offer warmed her heart, but the last thing Ronnie needed was Mom to see the true extent of this project. Or worse, to find out the truth about Lana and her job. *And* inadvertently tell everyone. "I'm fine, Mom. I have Hudson here, too. He's actually helping me." Not entirely a lie. By Hudson helping Colten paint out there, Ronnie's job of making the house presentable for sale *would* be easier.

"Okay." Marian sounded a little disappointed. "But if you need anything—"

"I will call you."

"And maybe don't wait an entire week to text me next time? I thought you'd ended up rolled over in a ditch or kidnapped. By mountain men, you—"

"You're being a little dramatic," Ronnie interrupted.

"Maybe a little."

It took another five minutes to successfully hang up the phone. Marian kept remembering one more thing. "You're sure you're not out there to elope with some cowboy?" The last thing she needed was a distraction. Mom's tirade had reminded her more than ever that Ronnie needed to focus on this project so she could impress Lana and get her job back.

Though Mom's idea was preposterous, it didn't stop Ronnie from picturing Colten's face. She shook it away. "I'm *not* eloping. Bye, Mom!"

CHAPTER 10

olten

It'd been a long day herding cattle to the summer pasture. Most of them cooperated, but a handful were set on doing their own thing. More than once a steer to two made Colten turn his horse to keep them from dashing back home. Hudson had been doing much of the same. Sometimes it took both of them teaming up to keep the fractious herd in line.

The back of his neck felt on fire; it'd teach him to forget his hat. A few small clouds had threatened much-needed rain, but never delivered. Colten, wiping his forehead on his sleeve, would've been glad for at least a bit of shade. But the hot wind took them and shredded the high bits of gray vapor into mares' tails.

His faced heated, and not from the sun, when he remembered his encounter with Ronnie this morning. Knowing she was already awake and working, he'd been upstairs searching his room for his work shirt, dressed only in a pair of jeans, when he realized the shirt he wanted was downstairs in the dryer. As he reached for the door, Ronnie practically fell into his arms, wrapped in nothing but a towel.

"Sorry!" she practically screamed. "Wrong room!" She scurried across the hall and slammed the door, and he'd hightailed it down the stairs and to the laundry. Getting to the ranch with nothing on his head but a ball cap from the back seat was a sad substitute, but Colten couldn't bring himself to run back into the house.

Rattled, remembering something as basic as a Stetson was the furthest from his mind. His pulse still hadn't calmed.

"Why don't we grab a bite at The Watering Hole?" Hudson suggested, bringing him back to the present. To the pasture filled with steers and away from the house filled with an alluring designer. "Heard Bev is having a special tonight on pulled pork sandwiches. We could grab a spot on the deck."

"Sounds good to me." Anything to keep him away from that house.

"Good. I'll text Ronnie. I feel bad. I've hardly

shown her around at all. She didn't exactly pick the best time to come."

Well, duh. Of course he would invite his visiting sister to join them. "Sure. Show her you're doing your best. Want me to ask Jed too? Ronnie seemed to get along with the kid." Too bad he couldn't think of anyone else to include. More people might help him keep his distance a little easier.

"Hey, with your light schedule this week, maybe you could sneak some sightseeing in for me? Make sure she doesn't work her entire vacation away. At least take her around town if you can?"

Colten swallowed. There didn't seem to be an easy way out of this one. He yanked his reins and tried for a benign smile. "For you buddy, I can do that."

The Watering Hole was almost as busy on Monday nights as on the weekends, but Hudson had called ahead to save them a table on the deck. Colten agreed to meet them rather than ride along. He'd planned to pick up Jed, but the kid had other plans and declined free food. Colten also had a call to make before he went in.

In the graveled parking lot of the riverside restaurant, his hand shook. He leaned against the truck, trying to look as if he were having a casual conversation. But it was more for support to ensure his legs didn't give out. His old boss had told him, 'Call whenever you're ready to come back.' But after more than two years, maybe he'd changed this mind, deciding too much time had lapsed.

Most of all, making this call meant taking a serious step toward leaving Starlight.

"Colten Livingston, as I live and breathe!" His old boss, Ralph, boomed from the other end, near excitement in his tone. "How you been, man?"

Colten filled Ralph in on the past two years, brushing over the details of his dad's passing. Mrs. Miller walked between Colten's truck and the fence lining the parking lot. He tipped his hat at her, turning away to keep his conversation as quiet as he could.

"He lived longer than anyone expected, doctors included. Can't ask for more than that." Ralph had only been his boss for three months before Colten had to walk away from his dream job to move back to Starlight.

"You've got impeccable timing. Haven't had any openings in months, but just last week a guy handed in his notice. His wife's having a baby. Insisted they move closer to family. Down Colorado, if I remember right."

The news struck a chord with Colten. With his mom leaving for Denver, and only Uncle Joe, Aunt Violet, and a few cousins left in Starlight, did it really matter where he went? He might never have a family of his own to share with relatives anyway. Once Danica left, he swore off ever getting married again. So, why was some voice in him questioning his strong resolve? Colten's musing nearly let the next bit of information from Ralph slip past him.

"I'll email you the application," Ralph said. "Formalities, you know. But you put I recommended you. And get it sent over yesterday. We've got half a dozen rangers trying for the spot. You're the only one I can vouch for."

"Thanks, Boss." He'd always called Ralph that, even after he'd been gone for six months and Ralph called to check in the first time, hoping Colten was coming back to work soon. "I'll get the paperwork filled out tonight."

On his way to the deck, Colten dropped his cell in his shirt pocket and adjusted his Stetson. Tingles of excitement raced through him at the prospect of landing the job for a second time. He loved Glacier National Park. Something about the atmosphere, the wilderness, the variety of animals roaming the thousands of mountainous acres spoke to him in a way no other place ever had.

He found Hudson and Ronnie at a table near the railing overlooking the water. They'd both ordered a beer on tap and were halfway through a glass. It intrigued Colten that Ronnie drank beer instead of some fruity drink in a fancy martini glass.

"Sorry, we didn't order one for you yet," Hudson said as Colten took a seat opposite. It put him next to Ronnie. Too late to move now. "Didn't want it getting warm."

"Not a problem." The waiter saw him fall into his cast-iron chair and hurried over to take his drink order. It'd been a while since he enjoyed a beer after a hard day's work, so Colten followed suit. A celebratory drink, though only Colten knew that.

About to tell Hudson about the call, he stopped. What would Ronnie think? The question rattled him. Why should he care? In a little more than a week, she'd head back to Chicago, return to her glamorous city life. His mom would move away. So, what was holding him back from sharing the news?

"I was telling Ronnie about that steer that decided to get stuck today. Mud up to our heels," Hudson said, picking up the story somewhere in the middle. "Or at least we *thought* he was stuck. He was playing us." Hudson nodded toward Colten. "Colten has the muddy jeans to prove it."

"Really?" Ronnie said. She reared back to take him in. "I didn't see him when he came home today."

The word *home* struck Colten more than her gaze did, making his stomach flop in a weird way. Before he could think about it too much, his drink arrived, and he took a refreshing gulp.

"You didn't track mud through the house, did you?" she continued.

"No." Colten set his sweating glass down and eased back into his metal chair. "I showered at my cabin. Left them there on the ranch."

"Hey, I'll be right back." Hudson scooted his chair back when he recognized someone. "I need to chat quick with Chuck. Colten, tell her about the Bighorn mountains."

"The what mountains?" Ronnie lifted her glass to the waitress, mouthing, *Another?*

"The ones with the snowcaps? Those're the mountains you see out the bedroom window. The room you're sleeping in now. There's a national forest surrounding them, but the drive's quite something. Not sure a city girl would appreciate it much, though."

"You seem set on believing it's impossible I'd enjoy anything about the wide-open spaces. Why is that?"

"Just don't seem the type." It was unfair to compare her to Danica in that way, but Colten couldn't seem to help it. Eager to shift the subject before he said something to earn him a menacing glare instead of a cute one, he added, "What were you really doing at the storage unit lot? When we first met?"

"Told you."

"No." Colten shook his head. "I let you off the hook in front of your brother the other night. You owe me."

"I do not."

"Does Hudson know about your little fender bender?"

"I was lost. Don't ask me why I turned into a crowded parking lot instead of an empty one. I don't know. I was disoriented, okay?"

The defense in her tone warned him to drop the subject. She had something to hide, he knew that for certain by her reaction. "Maybe it means you're thinking about sticking around?" Colten's heart jumped a little harder than it had been when he was pounding in fence posts the other day. Why did the answer matter to him?

"Nah, I don't think so."

"But you packed up your stuff anyway?"

"That doesn't mean—" But Ronnie cut herself off, her eyes growing wide.

Part of the secret came out, and for a moment Colten felt victorious. But the desperate look in her eyes took his pride down a notch. "Please, don't say anything." Ronnie fiddled with a cocktail napkin, folding and unfolding it. "Hudson'll worry, and I don't need him to. Everything's fine. I just need to line up a new apartment, that's all."

"Why bring it all to Wyoming? Chicago can't be short on storage units."

Ronnie's gaze stayed fixed on her menu. "It's a long—"

"Sorry about that." Hudson dropped back into

the booth. "Chuck has a four-wheeler I want. Made him an offer."

"Four-wheeler?" Ronnie asked, stumbling on her words. "What would you need that for?"

Hudson laughed then. "Look around you, Sis. What wouldn't I need that for? It'll be nice to have on the ranch for odds jobs, like fixing fences. But there are trails everywhere, and mountains. So much to explore."

Colten could understand why Ronnie didn't want to worry her brother. He was a changed man from the Hudson Ross who arrived a couple of years ago. Back then, he was solemn faced, didn't say much, didn't smile at all, and worked on the ranch until he was ready to drop into bed. Now, Hudson smiled. He laughed. If he knew his sister was homeless, it'd consume him until he fixed the problem.

"I've never ridden a four-wheeler before," Ronnie said.

"Well, if Chuck takes my offer, maybe we'll have to go. Colten has one, too. The three of us could hit one of the trails. If you think the view from the house is nice, wait until you see it from the top of one of those rolling hills."

"Sure," Colten jumped in, as Ronnie seemed short on words. His fault, of course. He'd try mending things later, when she might not be so resistant. Would it be too much to hope she'd eventually open up to him?

He still couldn't figure out why it mattered. Tonight he'd fill out that application. With any luck, in a couple of weeks he would be moving. Best to keep his distance for a few days. Even if—by some odd chance—Ronnie did decide to stay in Starlight, he wouldn't be here.

CHAPTER 11

THE NEXT COUPLE of days seemed a blur to Ronnie. She spent most of her time finishing up the demo work. Pulling out trim, removing the last scrap of wallpaper in the dining room, ripping up the kitchen's vinyl flooring. She even managed to paint one living room wall, though she wasn't sure about the color now that it was up.

She'd seen very little of Colten. He spent his mornings at the ranch and afternoons painting and staining outside. During an afternoon break in which he had disappeared, Ronnie wandered toward the end of the driveway, right before it snaked left into a huddle of tall trees. From here, the house looked completely different than when she'd first seen it.

The impression then was that it seemed . . . rundown. Almost sad. Not neglected in a way trash and weeds overran the place. But in a way that said its inhabitants were tired. That life had hit an extra rough patch and it didn't want to let up.

Now, with its soft yellow siding and half the window sills boasting a fresh coat of white gloss, the place looked as if someone had given it new life. She wondered if someplace in town sold fresh flowers. Ernie had some potting soil at the store, and if she remembered correctly, the spider-infested shed had a couple of pots she could clean up. When those final touches were finished, any new buyer would scoop it up.

"Hope you're saving the fireplace demo for me."

Colten caused her to jump. She expected to find him in a truck, but in focusing on the house, she felt caught off-guard having him hop off a horse behind her. One whose long muzzle was only a few feet away from her face. She'd never been this close to any horse before and wasn't sure what to do. She cautiously raised her hand toward the tip of its nose.

"She'd like you a whole lot better if you had an apple," Colten said. He pulled a small one from his shirt pocket and handed it over.

Ronnie struggled to ignore the heat of his touch.

For nearly two days she'd hardly seen, much less been near, him. Strange to think that she'd missed him. It didn't make any sense. Then to have Colten showing up on a horse in that irresistible cowboy hat and those Wrangler jeans, was scrambling her ability to reason.

"Go on." He grinned. "Dolly's waiting."

Ronnie slowly raised her hand, apple sitting in her palm. Dolly scooped it up, her soft nose tickling against Ronnie's hand as she crunched on the apple, the entire thing gone in under a minute. She nudged for more.

"You just made a new friend."

"I'll take all I can get." She meant to sound funny, but the words tasted sour in her mouth. She only had Reese, really. Ronnie's long hours focused on chasing her dreams had left as much time for new friendships as it had for dating.

Maybe something needed to change.

"You ready?"

"Ready?"

"Your tour of Starlight." He stepped back and nodded toward the horse. "Hudson made me promise I'd take you away from work tonight."

Any inkling that Ronnie'd had about him wanting to do this for *her* left in that moment. It was simply a favor for Hudson. "Let me guess. *He's* working late again."

"They suckered him into helping with the addition for the elementary school." Colten hopped up in the saddle, scooting forward and extending his hand down to Ronnie. "Starlight loves Hudson Ross."

"I'm starting to see why he never left." Ronnie took a step forward but tossed a hesitant look back to the house. Becca was due back in a couple of days. She wanted to at least have a fresh coat of paint on *all* the interior walls before she showed up. "I shouldn't. I have plans to finish before I go shopping for materials. I need to paint, run the shop vac—"

"Get on this horse," Colten ordered, not giving her room for arguing. "You work too much. You need a good hard lesson in learning to relax a little."

Ronnie looked around, no sight of a second horse. This was officially a bad idea. Her ability to form intelligent words, or any words for that matter, seemed vastly diminished whenever Colten was too close. "But—"

"Ronnie? It's a double saddle."

She had noticed the two separate grooves, but still, it wouldn't put much space between them.

"Do you want to hurt Dolly's feelings?" The horse's ears perked at her name. "She's been looking forward to getting out all day, haven't you, girl?" Colten ran a hand along her sleek neck.

"Okay."

Ronnie took a cautious step closer to what she

thought they called the stirrup. She hated to ask, fearing Colten teasing her for being an uneducated city girl. But she wouldn't risk falling on her butt, or worse, hurting Dolly. "How do I . . . do this? Which foot? Wait." It all came out in a stammer. "How do I get up there? Don't we need a box or something?"

"Put your left foot in the stirrup." Colten pointed. "Now, grab my hand. I'll pull you up, standing, then you swing your other leg over. Think you can do that?"

From the ground, she took his hand. "We're about to find out."

With a deep breath, Ronnie followed instructions. Colten's grip was strong, reassuring her that he wouldn't let her fall. Ronnie slipped easily into the back of the double saddle on her first try. Her smile stretched her cheeks. "I did it!"

"Good job." Colten patted her thigh. Then as if in realization, drew his hand away. "Now, hold on." Colten waited for her to put her arms around him before he urged Dolly forward down the rest of the graveled drive, onto the road toward Starlight.

Ronnie asked, "They let people bring horses into town?" Trying desperately to distract herself from the warmth created with her hugging her arms around his waist. Was he feeling it, too?

"You're in Wyoming, darlin'. Of course we can. They even have a couple of places to park them."

Her skin tingled at his close proximity. Her cheek bumped Colten's back with every few steps Dolly took.

"*Park* them?"

Colten laughed, the vibration of it evident through his shirt, and the muscles under it pressed up against her chest. "You can tie the reins at a couple of places. There's water for them." Each rocking motion from Dolly's easy stride pushed her toward Colten, then away. He spoke and she heard him in a vibration that she felt to her toes. "But we're not going into town tonight."

"We're not?"

"Nope. Got something else in mind. Hudson wanted me to show you Starlight, and there's one spot that's perfect for that."

"Where?"

"Patience," he said, then advised, "And bounce with Dolly's stride or you'll be really sore tomorrow."

The sun dipped lower in the horizon, behind the rolling hills and a couple of the snow-capped mountains. Ronnie found it hard to look away. "It's beautiful."

"Just wait. We're going to pick up the pace so we don't miss the best sunset in Starlight."

Ronnie tightened her grip, and tried her best at *bouncing*, hopeful it would prevent her from falling. At least from falling off the horse. She wasn't so sure anything could keep her safe from falling for this cowboy.

When they crested the rise of a dirt trail, the view laid out from the vantage point stunned Ronnie into silence. The town of Starlight was lit up in the valley below. The sun painted the rolling hills with its golden hue. How many sunsets had she missed in Chicago? Ronnie wasn't sure she'd ever stopped long enough to watch one.

"This is breathtaking." Tears pricked the corners of her eyes but she felt too embarrassed to let Colten see them. She ducked her head into his back. "And you get to see this *every* day?"

"The city has its conveniences, plenty of shoe stores, and I'm sure a bunch of other benefits. But can it compete with this sunset?"

In this single moment, Ronnie couldn't imagine going back to Chicago. She'd slowed down more this past week than in the last three years working for Lana. Ronnie was still proud of the work she'd accomplished, but here she'd learned to unwind. To enjoy moments she might otherwise take for granted.

"We'll eat soon," Colten said. "But not until you've had a chance to watch the stars come out. I promise, you've never seen so many in your life as you will in about fifteen minutes." Deftly, Colten slid off the saddle, the absence of his warmth leaving her empty. "C'mon." He reached up for her. "I brought a blanket."

"Are we having a picnic?"

"Well, Hudson said to make sure I fed his little sister, so Aunt Violet hooked us up."

Any hint of romantic intentions fled in that statement. Right, he was doing Hudson a favor. Nothing more than that.

"You have objections to a picnic under the stars?" he asked, seeing her frown.

"Nope." It sounded pretty perfect, actually.

Colten pulled a blanket from a saddle pack and spread it on the ground. "You're about to see why they call this town Starlight." He folded a second one on top of it. Ronnie was happy for that, as goosebumps were already forming on her arms with the sun gone. "Have a seat."

As Ronnie slipped off her sandals and settled onto the blanket, Colten unpacked a simple meal of sandwiches, chips, some fruit salad, and bottles of water.

He staged the food between them, building a barrier to keep them apart. Ronnie let go of all hope that he'd somehow longed to spend time together. That any of this might have been to impress. She settled into focusing on the emerging stars. At first there were only a handful shining to the east. But as the seconds ticked by, the sky filled with not just stars, but entire galaxies. Her neck already ached from craning it back to take in the vastness of the now-cobalt sky.

"Have a sandwich. Aunt Violet made chicken salad today. Best in the state."

"And here I thought you cooked," teased Ronnie.

"Only when there's no other option."

Ronnie took a bite and instantly moaned. "This is amazing!" She'd had chicken salad sandwiches before, but none that lit up her taste buds like this one. The mixture of flavor and texture was incredible. "Please tell me your aunt sells this by the gallon."

"We've all tried to talk her into opening her own catering business, but she's not interested. She likes cooking for the crew and has no interest to make it anything else." Colten reached for a sandwich of his own, their hands brushing in unexpected contact. Ronnie's skin zinged with feeling. *Did he really not feel that?*

"What brought you back here?" Ronnie asked, desperate to keep conversation going. Without it, she'd probably do something stupid like try to kiss him. The last thing she needed to do was embarrass herself this far from the house. That walk back in wedge sandals wouldn't be fun.

"To Starlight? My dad."

At first, Ronnie thought he wouldn't say more. Colten didn't seem one for giving up a lot of information, but he surprised her by continuing without prompt.

"He was diagnosed with prostate cancer. Refused to move anywhere with a decent hospital for treatments. I moved back so Mom and I could take turns driving him to Gillette. Take care of things at home. Dad was heavily involved in the ranch until all that. Co-owner, actually. But Joe bought him out to help with finances."

Ronnie was afraid to ask another question. Colten had shared more tonight than in the last week combined. But she did it anyway. "What were you doing before you moved back?"

Colten pulled off his hat and ran a hand through his hair. "Park ranger. At Glacier."

"Glacier National Park?" She turned toward him. He'd tossed his hat onto the edge of the blanket.

"That's the one."

"You prefer being a park ranger to a rancher?"

"Is it hard to believe that I love roaming over fifteen hundred preserved acres of wilderness?"

She studied him, or maybe that was an excuse to keep staring in those eyes. "No, I can see it." The harder question caught in her throat. Ronnie had only met Becca, not Colten's dad, and she could only assume his mom was moving to Denver for one of two reasons. "How long has he been gone?"

He broke eye contact, returning his attention to the valley below. "Four months next week."

"I didn't know. Colten, I'm so sorry."

"Thanks. Me, too."

As the millions of stars filled the sky, they sat in silence and watched. Ronnie felt certain she'd never seen a more beautiful place in all her life. "Why don't more people live here?"

"It's a rough life at times," Colten answered. "Especially come winter. Not everyone's cut out for what it takes to make it here." His boot tip touched her toes. "Some people run away pretty quick once they realize life isn't all that glamourous." Bitterness tipped those words.

"Who was she?"

Colten pushed up to his knees and started packing the leftover sandwiches. "Doesn't matter anymore."

Ronnie cringed, regretting the bold question. He'd opened up to her more than ever before, but maybe she'd pushed too far. What right did she have, digging into his past hurts when she was still lying about hers? In that moment, she yearned to tell Colten everything. But he'd already packed their leftovers into his saddle bag.

"No dessert?" she asked, her voice almost too quiet to hear.

"There might be some in the fridge at home."

Home. It had an odd familiarity to it. For one foolish moment, she dared to consider what it might be like to really be going home with Colten. To live in that house together, to someday raise a family.

"Mom said she'd call you tomorrow, something for the house," Colten said, shattering her silly fantasy. “I think she’s extending her stay in Denver, too.”

“Okay.” Tomorrow Colten would go back to avoiding her, no longer doing Hudson a favor. It seemed foolish dreams were nothing more than an opportunity for disappointment when you were the only one thinking them.

CHAPTER 12

onnie

Ronnie wasn't about to argue. Despite Colten's shift in mood and the untouched pie in the fridge, today he was inside. "It's time to take this subway tile down." He'd picked up a sledgehammer. "I've been waiting patiently, but it's the last demo thing on your list. I peeked."

Ronnie had to agree on the tile. "You really don't like that tile, do you?"

"Nope."

About to ask what he might like instead, Ronnie was stopped by his lifting the sledgehammer and swinging. Shattered tile clattered to the floor, echoing dully against the exposed subfloor. "We really should be using a hammer drill," she hollered over the noise. "It's easier!"

"This is more fun."

"But—" Her phone rang, the single bar indicating her signal was dangerously low. "Oh! I need to take this." She raced toward the back door.

"Ronnie?" Colten called out.

She poked her head around the doorway of the kitchen. "Yeah?"

"Use the ladder this time."

Sending him a salute, she shuffled outside and scurried up the ladder he still had propped against the porch. "Reese, hold on!" Ronnie hoped her friend could hear, and she'd wait as she climbed the ladder. Some days the signal was strong. Others, like today when there was a cloudy sky, things were iffy.

Halfway up, Ronnie stopped. "Reese? Can you hear me?"

"You sound out of breath! Have you been running?"

"Just to some good reception." A little breeze brought Ronnie back to her surroundings, and she found herself hugging the ladder, coiling her arms around the rungs like a pretzel. "Did you find the flooring?"

"Do you want the good news first or the bad?"

Of course there'd be bad news. There always was. "Better shoot me the bad. Rip off the Band-Aid."

"I found your floor but . . . What is going on out there?"

"Colten's inside smashing tile. He insisted on using a sledgehammer."

"Um, who's Colten?"

"Son of my client. Irritating cowboy type who's being uncharacteristically helpful today." Ronnie didn't want to keep on about Colten, though. "You found my flooring? That sounds like good news."

"It would be, but it's in Cheyenne."

"Oh." Ronnie tried to remember how far Cheyenne was from Starlight. "Roughly four-hour drive each way, huh?"

"Yeah."

If Ronnie made a trip to Cheyenne, she'd need a truck and a complete list of things that couldn't be found in Starlight. The chance of anyone delivering materials from that distance was unlikely. Not without a hefty fee. A day away would cost her too, even with Becca's extended house-hunting tour in Denver. "Dang. Well, what's the *good* news?"

"There are two different stores that have your laminate. Neither one has enough, but between the two, they do. I found a twenty-percent off coupon at one of the stores but it has to be used by closing tomorrow."

"Any chance they deliver?"

"Nope."

A fly buzzed by and Ronnie swatted at it until

the ladder began its wobble again. Today was windier than any other Wyoming day she'd experienced. "Wait, how is any of this good news?"

"Because I came up with a solution to get your flooring to you without any additional cost. Plus, you won't have to give up a day to get it."

"Really?"

"I'm flying into Laramie tonight to pick it up myself. Cheyenne's only a tiny jog from there, but I couldn't find any direct flights."

"Reese, I couldn't possibly ask you—"

"You didn't. I offered. Besides, it sounds like you're having an adventure and I want in. I've always wanted to meet that hunk of a brother of yours, too. You keep hiding him from me whenever he visits."

"He's only been through Chicago once." Ronnie left out that he'd been engaged at the time.

"I'm already at the airport, about to board. If I don't come, my favorite running shoes will end up in Wyoming without me."

"Reese, you know I can't pay you. I'm pretty much doing this for free. But I can offer you a place to sleep." She hoped Becca wouldn't mind the extra person in the house if she wasn't paying for Reese to be there. Probably best to give them a heads up.

"I didn't say anything about being paid," Reese reminded her. "I'm only there for the weekend. Lana thinks I have a stomach bug."

Ronnie cringed. What had she started? The last thing she needed was to be the cause of Reese, her only friend, getting fired.

"My flight lands this afternoon," Reese added. "Gives me plenty of time to get the flooring and anything else you need. Text me a list. I'll drive it up tomorrow morning."

"You. Are. Amazing."

"I do what I can." Chatter sounded in the background, something about a flight boarding. "Gotta go. See you tomorrow!"

Ronnie felt a weight lift at the thought of Reese coming to help, even if she could only offer a day or two. Reese was magic when it came to hunting for odd materials. Ronnie could share her vision and let her friend tell her where to find everything.

When Ronnie returned inside, she felt revived.

"Sounds like help is on the way." Colten stood amid a pile of shattered tile. Chips and hunks of it lay at his feet. He'd made fast work of the task. The roto hammer was nowhere in sight, but the sledgehammer leaned against the bare fireplace. "Windows are open. And with that breeze . . . Hey, I'm not *that* irritating."

"Wow, I didn't think that sledgehammer idea would work," Ronnie said, focused on the larger pile of fireplace debris and ignoring his last remark. If their playful banter started up again, it'd only confuse her more. Best to keep things less complicated.

"Maybe it's messier." She kept her eyes on the amount of dust he'd kicked up. "But not like we were going to use that gross tile for anything else, right?"

"Wasn't in my plan." When Ronnie could salvage materials from a demo, she did. That's how she'd ended up with half the items in her storage unit. But this stuff had been in such rough shape to begin with, she didn't blame Colten for demolishing it so thoroughly. Ronnie wished she could sneak away to her storage unit to grab some samples, but that would surely raise suspicion.

"Good. My dad would be pretty happy about this."

The smile that warmed his face softened her resolve. Could they actually be friends? Certainly they'd never be anything more. But Ronnie could live with having another true friend. "I'd offer to whip up a batch of those brownies I still owe you and Jed, but I'm curious about that dessert in the fridge."

"You can make brownies tomorrow. I'm bringing Jed back by. Told him he could help paint." Colten pulled out a shop rag from his Wranglers' back pocket and wiped away beads of sweat from his forehead. "Who's your friend?"

"Reese," Ronnie answered. "She and I work together." At least that statement wasn't a complete lie. They *would* be working together the whole time

Reese was here. It'd be like Ronnie having her own assistant. Except she wouldn't yell at her the way Lana did or talk down to her if she made a mistake.

"You okay? You look like you bit into a lemon."

"Just thinking about something you said," Ronnie admitted. "About Lana."

"May not have been kind, but I only say things I mean."

For the first time, Ronnie didn't feel so desperate to impress Lana. Maybe her design career options were quashed in Chicago. If they were, Ronnie would have to live with that. But she'd had a blind eye to Lana's impossible treatment of all her employees. Many accepted the cutthroat environment as part of climbing the ladder. Others loved the idea of getting a little screen time from the show. Ronnie didn't know what to think anymore.

"Where'd you leave the broom?" Colten asked, shaking her back to the present.

"In the kitchen, next to the fridge." Putting thoughts of Lana out of her head, Ronnie decided to take a new approach. She opened her laptop and sat in the middle of the room, assessing it from a new angle. Her previous choices, even in paint color, had been too modern. Too sleek. Too city for this charming small country town.

"What are you doing?"

"Making some changes," Ronnie replied. She no longer liked any of the light fixtures she'd picked out for the ceilings. Luckily any preliminary design plans were fixable. She had time to find new ones in stock in Cheyenne if she focused.

"You have money in the budget for that?" Colten hovered behind her, bending to better look at the screen. His proximity caused her to breathe a little faster. Ronnie pushed away the observation. There was work to be done. Time to focus.

The question reminded Ronnie that Becca'd be calling today, though she didn't know why. She suspected Colten might have been checking up on her and sending progress reports. But unless fishing in the evening was frowned upon . . .

"I like a challenge." Ronnie hadn't purchased most of the materials she picked out. Not without knowing how to get them to Starlight inexpensively. "In college, we had to decorate an eight-by-eight space on a hundred-dollar budget. The staging space had just a cutout for a window; its three walls were plywood. Just a big open room."

"What did you turn that into?" Colten asked as he swept up the shattered tile onto a dust pan.

"I turned mine into an office space. Found a writing desk on a curbside someone was going to throw away. A stool at a thrift store, added a cushion I sewed myself. Talked a small paint dealer into giving me a bargain on some overstock paint." Ronnie shrugged, shy all of a sudden. "I spent ninety-eight dollars and twenty-two cents. Got an A, too."

"Impressive."

She waited for the next page of light fixtures to load on her laptop. "It taught me a lot. That project won me the internship with Lana." Ronnie'd always beamed with pride, adding that last detail when she told her story. But this time, it sat sour in her mouth. "I've learned a lot working at her firm."

"Who are you trying to convince?" Over his shoulder Colten asked, "Me or yourself?"

RONNIE SPENT the remainder of the afternoon and into the evening fixing her design. Colten hovered over her shoulder on his breaks, asking a question here and there about her new plans. If it hadn't been for him shoving a chicken salad sandwich under her nose on one of those breaks, she might've forgotten to eat.

How had she been so blind to her own instincts? Her need to impress Lana had ruled over this design project, and now every bit of it needed scrapping.

The house suddenly felt too stuffy for Ronnie. "I'm going to take a short break." Hurrying upstairs, she tossed on a hooded sweatshirt and grabbed her flats. Though the sun was starting to disappear, the moon tonight would be nearly full, easily enough light for a brief walk. Ronnie wasn't fooling herself.

As she stepped down the hallway, it came to her; she needed out of the house and away from Colten, who'd done nothing but scramble her thoughts since they met.

In socks, she tip-toed down the stairs, relieved to find the living room empty of him. He was probably throwing the last of the tile trash into the dumpster. Tomorrow it would be picked up for good. She took the opportunity to sneak out the kitchen door and sat on the back steps of the wraparound porch to slip on her shoes. This magnificent porch that spanned three sides of the house, she had to admit, was one of her favorite features. Especially now that it offered an escape route.

Ronnie wished she'd paid more attention to the trail when they fished in the daylight. Briefly, she considered borrowing Lou, but that required either sneaking her out with a treat or actually asking permission. She didn't want Colten's company right now. Her emotions were warring inside. The lie was too much to keep up. And Colten was a danger right now. If she didn't tell *someone* the truth, she might burst.

Colten rounded the corner from the front of the porch. "Going somewhere?"

"Where—"

"You're loud enough to wake a hibernating bear."

"And here I thought I'd make a good ninja."

Colten laughed, a low rumbling sound that

caused tingles to dance up her arms as he approached, his boots echoing off the wooden planks in slow, deliberate steps. Lou trotted beside him, tail wagging.

"Hey, girl." Ronnie distracted herself with the furry, lovable creature. Hugging Lou helped ward off the dread that tangled inside her. "I was going to steal Lou for a walk, but obviously I make a horrible robber."

"That you do." Colten leaned against a porch pillar. "If you wanted to take a walk, why didn't you just say so?"

Ronnie felt her heart leap into her throat. Was he suggesting what she thought he might be? The two of them. A moonlit walk? Alone? "I just needed some air. Figured Lou knew the way."

"Well, Lou's not the only one."

"I really wanted to be alone."

"Me, too." Colten removed his hat and tossed it onto a nearby rocking chair. Running a hand through his hair to loosen it up, he joined Ronnie on the steps and offered her a hand. "The stream is prettiest during a full moon. C'mon."

"I—"

"It's just a walk." Ronnie stared at the outstretched hand, safer than looking into those dangerous blue eyes. "I promise, I'll protect you from bears."

"B-bears?"

"I'll keep you safe."

Ronnie placed her hand in his, and let him pull her to her feet. At his touch, sparks ignited between their fingers, like an electrical current. It was her last chance to turn around, but her feet carried her forward.

CHAPTER 13

olten

LIVING IN WYOMING, Colten had seen many beautiful sights. Sights that stole his breath time and time again. But nothing quite compared to the sight of Ronnie bathed in the full moon's light, standing barefoot on a boulder along the stream.

"It's amazing!"

"It's no city skyline," he agreed.

"I think we've already established who has better night views." Ronnie sank onto a natural seat the flat boulder afforded, knees folded against her chest. Lou ran up behind her, standing guard. "I could sit out here all night, and . . ." Her head tilted back, looking directly overhead. "I just can't get over all these stars."

This particular boulder had always offered enough room for two. Knowing he shouldn't, Colten took a careful seat beside her. "You've just had all that city light blocking out the view."

"You really grew up here?" Ronnie's eyes were still locked on the sky above.

"Born and raised."

"I'm still surprised Hudson decided to stay." Ronnie scooped a stray hair away, tucking it behind her ear, revealing her soft neck illuminated by moonlight. "He wanted to travel the world three times over. Never the kind who sat still for long. Yet, he's been here two years. I get it now. This place, it changes people, doesn't it?"

"It has a way of captivating some people." It wasn't true of everyone; no. Otherwise Danica would still be here. At the thought of his ex-wife, Colten tensed. But one glance at Ronnie revealed a tear glistening at the corner of her eye.

"I don't deserve to be here."

"What?" Colten was confused how the conversation had taken such a sharp turn. Maybe it had to do with the reason she wanted to be alone.

"I hate working for Lana Bojanski." Tears came swiftly, surprising Colten. Ronnie's hands wiped them away as quickly. "There, I finally said it!"

"If you're looking to shock me, that won't do it."

Colten hoped his teasing might ease the tension, but it still hung in the air. "Hey, what is it?"

Ronnie shook her head before burying her face in her bent knees. Her body trembled. "This might be a good time to leave me alone."

"I'm not leaving you to the bears." She choked a laugh in reply. "C'mon, Ronnie. What is it? Whatever it is, it can't be that terrible. I already know you're between places to live. What else could possibly—"

"Lana fired me." Her head popped up, but her eyes stared out at the water. "The first time in three years I'm late, and I got fired."

"What?" Colten tensed at the revelation. As far as anyone knew, Ronnie was Lana Bojanski's assistant, so what was this lie she'd been spinning? What would Hudson think? What would his mom think? "Why would you lie about that?"

"I didn't want to tell Hudson I failed. He's so proud of me. I thought it would humiliate him in front of his friends." The sobs made some of her words hard to decipher, but Colten understood anyway. "I was embarrassed, too. Then your mom offered me the job—"

"Why'd you take it?"

"To prove I was worth giving a second chance. I thought if I could pull off this project on my own, in two weeks, Lana'd have to hire me back."

Part of Colten despised the deception, but a

bigger part hurt for Ronnie. She'd been holding on to such a big lie for a week. Every time someone mentioned the show or Lana Bojanski, she had to force a smile. Pretend everything was okay.

"I'm so sorry, Colten. I never meant to hurt anyone. I was hoping to get my job back and Hudson would never know the difference. He's been through so much. I didn't want him worrying about me. But I've made such a mess of . . . I never should've come."

At that, Colten's heart tugged. He wanted to tell her how glad he was she showed up. Maybe they *had* spent half their time at odds, but he'd enjoyed her company more than he cared to admit. His life was spent on a dull repeat before she came to Starlight.

But Colten didn't tell Ronnie any of that. He simply rubbed her back and let her cry until she seemed done.

"I don't know how you did it," Colten finally said. "I can only imagine what a picnic your boss was off camera."

"That last project was all I needed. I was so close to a promotion. If it had gone smoothly, they would've promoted me to designer. Given me my own assistant."

"What happens if you *can* get your job back?" Well crap, that was an insensitive question, Colten realized. But it was too late to take it back, and he *did* want to know the answer.

"I go back to being Lana's assistant, I guess. Put

in some more time to show the company I'm reliable. Hope for a promotion a year or two from now." Ronnie wiped at her eyes again, but she'd missed a stray tear. Colten brushed it away with his thumb. In that moment, he very much wanted to kiss her. Almost did.

Lou barked, catching them both off guard. "Lou, it's just a squirrel," Colten hollered.

"You sure it's not a bear?" Ronnie whispered, her body going rigid.

"Doubtful."

"Not reassuring." Lou trotted back to them, but the moment's tenderness was definitely gone.

"You want to hear the comical story of how I got fired?" Ronnie asked, a weak smile flashing in the moonlight. "My phone battery died when I fell asleep the night before with it on. I'd been searching for the perfect backsplash for a wet bar; Lana had given me an almost impossible pattern to find."

"That sucks."

"Oh, I'm just getting started." At least Ronnie laughed now. "I woke up and realized it was almost two hours past when I should've been on site. Panicked, of course. I switched the case to one of those full-charge ones. Hopped into the shower with my phone—to call Lana and explain."

"Oh, no."

"Oh, yes." The image of her phone thudding against the bottom of the tub and being soaked by the spray was still vivid and panic inducing. "I hopped out of the shower and stuffed it in a cereal bowl full of rice. When I left for work, my shirt was on crooked, my hair was still wet, rice kernels were flying everywhere. I'm sure I'm responsible for several bird deaths in my old driveway." Ronnie shook her head, but her smile began to grow. "Get this . . . my rear tire was flat."

"You're making that up."

"I swear, I'm not. Found a nail the size of a golf tee stuck in it. My elderly neighbor came outside, trying to talk me into calling Triple A. But I didn't have time for that. My saving grace was that his kids had recently given him a smartphone, which I borrowed. Left a voicemail for Lana, then downloaded the Uber app to catch a ride."

"But you were too late?"

"Stop getting ahead." Ronnie bumped him with her shoulder, rocking them both.

Colten came a little too close to rocking off the boulder. He saw Ronnie's eyes widen. "I'm good." He slipped his arm around her. "Continue."

"I got some nervous college kid driver. Probably his first day. He forgot to charge his GPS. We got lost."

Colten fought laughter but couldn't hold it back any longer. The absurdity of it all set him off. Ronnie started in with him, the sound as entrancing as music.

"Once we finally got there, well, you know the rest." She let out a heavy sigh. "And the cameras caught all of it. You know reality TV. It'll air in a couple of weeks for all the fans of the show to see, I'm sure."

"You think the universe might be trying to tell you something?" Colten asked. "Maybe you were in the wrong place in Chicago."

"Never thought of it that way," Ronnie admitted, resting her head on his shoulder.

It felt easy to pretend they were a couple. That Ronnie might be here to stay; that Colten didn't have bigger dreams to chase; that they might build a life together. But he'd entertained that fantasy once before. It left him heartbroken in the dust trail.

"You okay?" Ronnie lifted her head, concerned eyes meeting his.

"Fine."

"Colten, you tensed up." She wouldn't look away. "What is it?"

"It's a boring, sad story. You don't want to hear it."

"Can't be much worse than the one I just confessed to."

Colten didn't want to talk about Danica. That was in the past. She'd never come back to Starlight, and maybe that was one of the reasons he stayed. She'd shown her true colors, leaving the way she did, but if he moved anywhere else, what would stop her from tracking him down? Bringing unwanted drama into his life? "It's not nearly as entertaining as your story."

"Is it about your ex?"

"Ex-wife." Colten gave Ronnie a moment to digest that fact. Expecting it to affect her opinion of him in some way. "Let's just say that vows didn't mean much to her when Dad got sick. She moved back with me, but she didn't stay."

"I'm sorry, Colten."

"Anyway, when she left, she lied. Told me it was just to visit her mom. Two weeks later, I got the divorce papers in the mail."

"That's awful."

"It's in the past." After a lapse of silence, Colten hoped the questions about Danica were over for the night.

"You must think I'm a horrible person, for lying."

"I don't think that, Ronnie."

"But I have to tell Hudson the truth. And your mom."

"Mom isn't coming back until next week now. Tell her after you've finished your renovation. The way I see it, with the work you've done so far, she'll forgive you. She comes off tougher than a bear, but she has a soft heart. I promise."

"And what about Hudson?"

"He'll understand. Tell him." He hugged her shoulder tighter against him. "Soon."

A silence stretched between them for a moment, but it was filled with so many unspoken thoughts. Colten risked asking, "What do you want, Ronnie? Do you *want* your job back?"

Ronnie picked up a stone and tossed it into the water with the elegance of dropping a bowling ball. "I think so."

"Then finish the job you started. See what your prospects are. If she doesn't offer you a job back, then figure out a new path." He rubbed her shoulder tenderly. "Bright side, Hudson'll be proud that you're managing Mom's job on your own. Isn't that your dream anyway? Being your own designer?"

Ronnie threw another rock, her toss just as clunky as the last. "Yeah."

"You can't throw a rock into the stream like that." Colten scooted to his feet, knowing if they stayed perched on the boulder much longer, he *would* kiss her. They were both too emotional tonight to let that happen. "C'mon." He extended his hand. "I need to give you a lesson on skipping rocks."

"In the dark?" Ronnie reached up a hesitant hand.

"What dark? There's a full moon."

But her foot caught, and she tumbled. Her hands collided with his chest, and his breath stopped. Surely she could feel the erratic beating beneath her palms.

Slowly her head tipped back and her chocolate

eyes, more amber in this moonlight, met his. He should stop himself, stop this from happening. Hudson would kill him tomorrow.

RONNIE

"How do you skip a rock?" Ronnie asked, pushing off Colten's chest, taking a step back. She'd almost kissed him. What had she been thinking, coming out here in the moonlight with a handsome cowboy when her emotions were all over the place?

"You have to find one with a good flat surface."

If they kissed, would it even mean anything? With all the tears she'd shed in his presence, Colten might've kissed her merely out of pity. Then regret would overcome him, and she'd probably not see him for days. Colten had made it clear, more than once, that his looking after her only had to do with her being Hudson's sister.

"Maybe we should head back." After Ronnie's pitiful attempt to find a flat rock, she added, "It's getting late."

"Yeah, maybe you're right."

A pang of disappointment surprised her. Had she expected him to try changing her mind? If she did, she was hopeless. She waited for Colten to take the lead and was a little touched when he reached out his hand. "For your protection. It's dark in those woods."

"Bears."

"Exactly."

She'd be lying if she told herself she didn't enjoy holding his strong, calloused hand. It offered a feeling of warmth and protection. She only wished it promised the same of her heart.

"Lou, c'mon," Colten called. The pup lingered on the edge of the creek, either taking a drink or eyeing a fish.

"How'd you come up with her name?" Ronnie asked, hopeful to keep the conversation cleared of her pathetic life. If she kept him talking until they made it back, she might keep from embarrassing herself further.

"Named her after Louis L'Amour."

"Before you knew she was a *her*?"

"Something like that." Colten paused, holding back a low-hanging branch so she didn't have to duck. "Lou was meant to be a cattle dog, but she mixed up with a mean bull when she was three months old. Broke several ribs and punctured a lung."

Ronnie's heart ached for what Lou must have endured. "That's awful."

"Lou was a lost cause far as my uncle or anyone on his ranch was concerned. Even my mom told me she was too far gone, and she's got a softer spot for animals than I do. But there was something in Lou's eyes that told me not to give up on her."

Dang it. Ronnie really thought she was done crying tonight. She tightened her grip, lacing her fingers in his. They stopped again. "You took her in?"

"Took three separate surgeries. One of the vets even told me recovery was grim at best. Said she'd never be normal."

Ronnie's eyes found the flash of multi-colored fur whisking by them. "She seems pretty normal now." They were closer, but Ronnie had no clue which of them had taken a step. "You saved her."

"Really, I think Lou saved me. It all happened just a couple weeks after Danica left. Lou gave me purpose again."

"And you gave her a chance." Ronnie knew she should put some distance between them. But with their fingers interlocked, the sparks from their contact awakened all her senses. She put her hand against his chest, feeling the thrum of his heart. It beat as fast as her own.

He caressed her cheek, drawing her lips to his. Colten's kiss made her dizzy, like she was spinning in crazy circles and floating at the same time. Then it deepened. Her hand slipped behind his neck, pulling him closer until their bodies pressed together.

A bark from Lou brought them back to reality.

Her tail wagging, she came charging past them toward the clearing near the house.

"I-I shouldn't have done that," Colten stammered, stepping back. "That was a mistake."

Ronnie stepped away too, breaking their connection. Of course he was right. He'd been the calm one. The indifferent one. It was Ronnie who'd stepped up and kissed him. How stupid could she be?

Lou barked again, this time higher pitched. A doggy call of, *Come look!*

Dread washed over Ronnie. Who would they find when they emerged from the woods?

CHAPTER 14

Ronnie

SLEEP HAD ELUDED Ronnie most of the night. How on Earth was she supposed to sleep after a kiss like that? Her nerve endings still tingled. The sun illuminated the room through the sheer curtains. What would have transpired if Lou hadn't gone into a barking fit over a baby raccoon?

Not that it mattered. It didn't mean anything to Colten. He'd made that perfectly clear. A *mistake* he called it. A person only apologized for a kiss if they used poor judgment in allowing it to happen in the first place.

No matter how exhilarating it'd been, Ronnie figured now the only tack was taking the same stance: *a mistake*. It was the only way to protect her heart. It'd been a long time since she let anyone in. That had to be the reason for such poor judgment. That and her soft spot for rescue dogs. Who wouldn't have kissed Colten after hearing that story?

RONNIE HAD JUST FINISHED SHOWERING when her phone rang. "Reese!" She shoved open her second-story window and stuck her head out for better service.

In all her moonlight escapades last night, she'd completely forgotten her best friend—her only friend—and her flight into Cheyenne. The guilt just kept piling.

"I'm in Starlight!"

"What?" Ronnie pulled the phone away to check the time. "Reese, it's hardly eight." As it was, Ronnie felt late. But she'd needed the sleep, and she knew not much would happen until Reese arrived with the flooring anyway. At least that was better than admitting she'd been hiding in her room, waiting for Colten to head to the ranch. "When did you leave?"

"Four this morning, after a quick run. No traffic that way."

"You left the flooring in the back of the truck?" Ronnie asked, not willing to touch the running comment. "Overnight?"

"I got one of those trucks with a bed cover. You know, those fancy ones that slide and lock."

Ronnie was trying to do the math in her head, how much the upgrade must have cost. "Reese, that was a lot of money. I wish you had let me drive down there."

"Relax, Ronnie. I didn't pay for it. Derek did."

"Reese!"

"If he can afford to take women who aren't his girlfriend out to fancy five-star restaurants, he can afford to rent my truck."

"Oh, no!" Ronnie had never cared much for Reese's boyfriend of two years. Sadly, it didn't surprise her that he'd strayed. Perhaps her friend needed the escape as much as she did.

"Anyway, I've always wanted to drive a big truck. Ronnie, it's so much fun!"

Ronnie talked Reese through the directions to the house.

Before heading downstairs to meet the woman rolling up the hill in a massive truck, Ronnie shot Hudson a text, asking him to make some time tonight. She needed to tell him the truth. Colten was right about one thing last night: Hudson would understand; she realized that now.

Ronnie met Reese on the front porch. For such a petite thing who hardly came to Ronnie's shoulder, her hugs were vise-grip worthy.

"It's so beautiful out here, Ronnie!" Reese spun a

full circle, sunshine reflecting in her sunglasses. When she stopped, she pushed them to the top of her head. "I can see the appeal."

"Hey." Colten's voice sounded behind them. The screen door slammed shut. Lou had burst out like an ignited bottle rocket, and the pup made her usual morning laps around the house.

Ronnie's heart raced at the sound of his voice. She was sure she'd heard him drive off.

"You must be one of Ronnie's friends." Colten smiled and held out his hand when Ronnie failed to introduce them.

"Reese Calloway." Reese grinned and began a satisfied rocking motion back on her heels. Ronnie could tell it was a strong-arm handshake she was giving him. The surprise in Colten's wide eyes amused her.

"Colten Livingston."

"Ah," Reese said, sizing him up once she let his hand loose. "*You're* Colten." A wicked smile danced across her lips. Ronnie suddenly regretted ever mentioning him. It was a good thing Reese didn't know about that kiss.

"What exactly have you been telling her about me, Ronnie?" Colten teased. "Other than how utterly irritating I am?"

Ronnie couldn't believe how normal he was acting right now, as if last night never happened. How was it so easy for him to ignore a kiss that spun her world upside down? The answer wasn't one Ronnie liked dwelling on, but it had to be true. If Colten felt even half of what she did, he'd be avoiding her like the plague. Or stealing more of those kisses. Not standing here chatting, acting like nothing ever happened.

"*Irritating cowboy* is really the only scoop I got," Reese teased. Turning her attention to Ronnie, she added, "But we'll be having a talk about *that* later. You obviously failed to mention a few things. Like how handsome *some guys* are in a cowboy hat."

"Handsome?" Colten repeated, recovering now, if that smirk he wore was any sign. "Ronnie, you forgot to mention how handsome I am?"

And just like that, pesky butterflies held a circus in Ronnie's stomach. "Reese, come have a look inside." She moved around Colten and held the door open, desperate to put some distance between them. It was that or she just might throw herself into his arms and steal another kiss. Probably the last thing he really wanted right now.

"You ladies have fun." Colten tipped his hat. "I have to pick up Jed. We'll finish up the outside today. We'll try to stay out of your hair."

Ronnie felt a tiny pang of disappointment that Colten wouldn't be helping inside today, but it was for the best. It absolutely was. If she had to be around him all day, Reese would surely figure everything out. It was bad enough with all that teasing outside. But if Ronnie was to forget that kiss ever happened, space was exactly what she needed.

"So *THAT'S* YOUR COWBOY, HUH?" Reese asked once the fading motor of his four-wheeler announced Colten's departure. "He's hot!"

"He's not *my* cowboy," Ronnie shot back. "Please don't say that out loud again."

"If you don't want him, honey, I'm going to scoot on up to the front of the line." Reese craned her neck toward the bay window, as if she might get a glimpse of Colten disappearing down the graveled drive. Her friend certainly didn't seem hurt by Derek's infidelity.

"It's complicated," Ronnie finally admitted, though the idea of Reese immediately making a move on Colten, well, it unsettled her a bit.

"Complicated how?"

Ronnie retrieved her laptop and notes from the kitchen table, prepared to get to work. "He's Hudson's best friend."

"Ah, I get it." Reese pointed a finger and waggled it. "But Ronnie, a man like that isn't going to stay off the market for long. Just saying."

"I'm not moving here, you know," Ronnie countered. "I'll be heading back to Chicago next week." Last night she'd been unsure, but this morning it all seemed clear enough to admit out loud. Staying in

Starlight, well, it was just escaping. What would happen come winter? Would she be stuck and miserable? "How is Lana?"

"You know Lana. She's proud. Won't admit she's wrong. Ever. But she's been a bit of a mess since you left. Gone through two assistants, and I think the third was about to get the boot when I snuck out of the office yesterday. You made an impression, you know?"

"I don't know," Ronnie said. "Lana's pretty stubborn."

"Producers are eating it up, of course. If you really want your job back, I think the odds are in your favor. Even if Lana has a pride issue, the producers would convince her otherwise. It'd be great for ratings, you coming back and saving her reputation."

"Really?"

"I think if you gave it another week or two, she'd be begging you to come back. Maybe you'd get a raise!"

It certainly gave Ronnie a lot to think about.

"Well," Reese kept on with her news. "She regrets firing you right at the start of that celebrity project. It's already four days behind schedule. Everyone knows you were the one holding everything together, not Lana. She's spending more time apologizing than getting any work done."

At that news Ronnie hid a grin. "Enough about

Lana. Let's talk paint colors. Now that you're here, I need your help deciding what to do with the dining room. I'm not sure I like any of the samples I picked up."

Later, Ronnie could make a phone call. If Reese was telling the truth, Ronnie wouldn't have to start at the bottom again. That changed everything. Not unlike last night's Earth-shattering kiss.

CHAPTER 15

olten

THOUGH FRIDAY WAS Colten's day off, he'd been hard-pressed to say no when Uncle Joe asked him to help move the last herd of heifers to the summer pasture. Jed's face was puffed up so much from a bad case of allergies, Colten wondered how he could see at all. He'd been to the doctor and was stuck waiting for the medication to take effect.

He told Hudson he agreed to help because of Aunt Violet's blueberry pancakes. But being around Ronnie, trying to keep his cool, had him feeling as if his heart might pop out of his chest. When he said that kiss was a mistake, he meant it. Now he had to live with the memory of her lips dancing with his own. Which was why it certainly couldn't happen again.

It had been nice to leave Lou with Jed, though. Colten was doubtful she'd want to be around the cattle, but she sure loved that kid. It'd be good comfort for a miserable day. Lou was a great snuggler when life got tough.

"Could've left Lou at your mom's place, you know," Hudson said.

Hudson obliquely mentioning Ronnie knotted the guilt in Colten's stomach a little tighter. It was one kiss. They'd been caught up and got carried away. Colten kept telling himself there was no need to tell Hudson about last night in the moonlight. It was a one-time thing. And wouldn't happen again. Ever. It'd only cause him unnecessary strain learning about it now.

"They're painting today. Didn't want Lou causing any trouble. Imagine that tail brushing up against all those freshly painted walls. Your sister might ban me from the house if Lou painted paw prints across every floor." It was some sad excuse and Colten knew it.

"Did Ronnie's friend make it in okay?"

Glad for a change of subject, Colten told Hudson a little about the spitfire that was Reese. "I think you'd like her," he teased. "Doesn't seem like the type to sit still."

"Hmm."

Colten expected a little more of a reaction than that. Though he didn't know the full extent of Hudson's past, he knew his friend had been left at the altar. A week later he showed up on Uncle Joe's doorstep with a duffle bag and a desperation to work away his troubles. What was supposed to be a summer gig turned into a full-time position once Joe saw what an asset Hudson Ross was to the ranch.

In those two years, Colten hadn't known Hudson to entertain a single date, though he certainly had multiple offers.

"You need help finishing up the outside?" Hudson asked as they trotted along at the tail end of the lowing cattle.

The heifers were behaving better than the steers had last week. Less chasing made for a quicker job. Colten almost wished one would stray so he'd have an excuse for staying away from Ronnie longer. "If you want." Colten shifted his Stetson an inch farther off his forehead. "I was counting on Jed to come out, but that kid can't even see his hand in front of his face right now. Last thing he needs is to be outside all day."

"I'll head back once we're through here."

COLTEN WASN'T PREPARED for the sight that met him when he rolled into the driveway that afternoon.

The fading glow of the sun illuminated Ronnie on his front porch, her wavy hair pulled up into a messy bun, the sleeves of a two-sizes-too-big flannel shirt rolled up, splatters of paint on her bare arms. One on her cheek.

"That's Reese?" Hudson asked, hand frozen on the door handle.

Until Hudson mentioned her, Colten hadn't even noticed her on the porch. "Uh, yeah. That's Reese." Watching his friend's reaction in wonderment, Colten popped him lightly on the shoulder. "You gonna sit and gawk or go introduce yourself?"

"I smell like a steer who's spent the day bathing in mud."

"Then, go up and take a shower."

Hudson gave him a look. He pushed his door open, waved to the women on the porch, then darted around the side of the house to use the back door. Too bad Colten couldn't do the same before he approached Ronnie. It'd been a warm day, with the sun beating down through most of it.

"You want to see what we got done?" Ronnie asked, a glow in her eyes. She seemed more at ease than she'd been this morning. Maybe Reese was having that effect on her. Maybe that kiss, stuck in his mind on replay, was pushed completely out of hers.

"You did more painting." He nodded to the splotch on her cheek. Though his fingers wouldn't do much good on dried paint, he fought the urge to brush them against her soft skin. It would only make him want to kiss her again.

Best to stick around people, he decided. If left alone with Ronnie, he wasn't sure what would happen.

"Downstairs is all done!"

"You painted the whole downstairs?" Colten remembered her telling him about the living room. But it didn't sound as though they'd get much more done.

"Well, once we got going, we couldn't stop. Ernie had all the paint colors we needed. He's pretty resourceful for such a small operation. Even got him to give me a discount."

"Ernie never gives discounts."

"You just don't know how to sweet talk the man."

The delicious scent of something baking caught his nose. "You bribed him."

"I may have offered him a couple of my butterscotch brownies," Ronnie admitted. "But I didn't force him to do anything. And before you say anything, I made you and Jed your own pan."

"Surely, I've earned about three pans of my own by now."

"Don't push your luck." Ronnie poked at his chest.

Though they still stood on the plywood subfloor, the walls in the living room were now tinted a soft gray. A color Colten had to admit he really liked. He wouldn't have paired it with the cedar trim had he been left to this decision on his own. "Works well."

"You want to see the rest?"

"Let me grab a shower." He had to get those thoughts out of his mind. "I'll check out the damage after."

"Ha ha." Ronnie's eyes narrowed at him, her crinkled nose making her even cuter.

He needed to be on his best behavior or Hudson would figure out they had a secret. No reason for anyone else to know. He headed upstairs, but at the sound of giggling coming from below, he worried Ronnie might've shared details with her friend.

Ronnie called up after him, "Don't suppose a second pan of brownies could bribe you into helping us unload some boxes of flooring before you head upstairs?"

Hudson would still be showering, so Colten would do little more than wait his turn upstairs. He turned. "Sure."

"Wait 'til you see these walls with the new floor! That's tomorrow's project." Ronnie rubbed her hands together. A tell, Colten was learning, that meant she was working up the courage to ask a favor. "How busy are you and Jed tomorrow?"

"I might have some time, but I doubt Jed'll be up for much." He briefly explained, "Allergies." He was touched by the genuine concern showing in Ronnie's eyes.

"He didn't get stung by a bee or something, did he?"

"That's what I thought too, but Aunt Violet said he picked up a new allergy this year. Some kind of pollen or something." Colten followed the women out to the truck and waited while Reese lowered the tailgate.

"The flooring's a little tricky," Ronnie explained. "Snaps together, but I've learned it helps to have a crew staged around a room this size to hold it in place until it's all down. Think Hudson might be able to help? You know more about what's going on at the ranch and around town than I do."

"I'll see if we can sneak away a couple hours early." Colten noticed how close Ronnie'd moved and instantly worried, knowing he stank. He reached for the first box and slid it toward him, then carried it into the kitchen where he stacked it along the far wall.

Once they were finished, he excused himself. "I better grab a shower." His eyes traveled to the paint smears on her arms. He wanted to tease her about it, but teasing had gotten him into this mess. Instead he rushed upstairs before she could affect him any more than she already had. The kiss had been the biggest mistake of all, he realized. If he hadn't kissed her, he wouldn't feel the desperate need to do it again.

CHAPTER 16

onnie

RONNIE'S ALARM sounded much too early the next morning, but Reese was only here for three days. They had to make the most of every minute they could. They'd been up late, convincing Colten and Hudson to help install the new light fixtures, change out the grungy outlet covers, and hang new curtain rods.

The project would never have come together without their help. She'd make sure Becca knew just how much everyone else had done. Ronnie could never take all the credit herself. Not the way Lana did.

Thoughts of her old boss made her cringe. She'd

stupidly placed that call yesterday when she thought she wanted her old job back. With any luck, Lana'd delete the message and never bother Ronnie again.

A soft knock drew Ronnie's gaze to the paneled door. She imagined Reese had showered and probably spent an hour working already, searching for their finishing touch materials.

"You *are* awake."

Ronnie rubbed sleep from her eyes, horrified that Colten stood in her doorway, looking ruggedly handsome in his Wranglers, and here she sat in pajamas with hair probably sticking up in every direction, smudged makeup beneath her eyes. "Did you need something?" Too late to close the door in his face now.

Last night had been oddly wonderful. The four of them had fallen into easy routine, as if they'd been fixing up houses together for months rather than only a day. She'd let her guard down near Colten, flirting more than she knew she should. At least her morning appearance would likely scare him off.

"Aunt Violet insisted I bring my guests for breakfast at the ranch."

A yawn escaped, but as tempting as falling back into bed for another hour sounded, Aunt Violet's breakfast sounded even better. If her menu was on par with her chicken salad sandwiches, Ronnie didn't want to miss out. "Give me ten minutes."

"Better hurry," Colten said to the closing door.

"Doesn't last long around a table filled with hungry ranch hands."

Ronnie blazed through a quick shower, then dabbed on a little makeup. She ran the blow dryer through her hair once, hardly enough to dry it, and ended up sticking the damp mess up in a bun.

As suspected, Reese was downstairs on her laptop, looking completely put together. "It's the time difference," she said, as if that explained everything. "Chicago's an hour later."

"Right."

Heavy footsteps sounded on the porch. Hudson poked his head in through the kitchen door. "You ladies ready?"

Guilt twisted in Ronnie's stomach. She'd put off talking to Hudson last night. He looked much too happy and carefree to drop the bomb and bring down his good mood. She convinced herself that if he could see her in her element, the news might be easier to digest when she did tell him. But the guilt of holding on to the secret for another day kept her awake half the night. Today, Ronnie was determined to pull him aside and spill the truth, no matter how much it sucked.

Ronnie expected to ride over in Colten's truck or even to follow separately. But instead, two four-wheelers waited at the bottom of the back steps, engines idling. Ronnie met the daring look Colten tossed over his shoulder, one he quickly seemed to turn around when Hudson glanced in his direction. Colten didn't think she'd get on, did he?

Reese squeezed Ronnie's arm and leaned in toward her ear. "Go get cozy with your cowboy."

"He's not—" But Reese had already flown down the steps and hopped on the four-wheeler Hudson was revving. Left with no other choice, Ronnie slipped into the seat behind Colten.

"Better hold on," Colten said over his shoulder, his lips much too close. "It's a bumpy ride."

Ronnie tried preparing herself as she slid in closer and wrapped her arms around his waist. The fireworks erupting throughout her body still unnerved her. It was getting easier, imagining that this was somehow her new normal. That maybe she and Colten could be together. Even Hudson and Reese seemed quite at ease with each other.

They zipped down the gravel road, both going slow enough that the bumps didn't dislodge anyone. The wind tried to rip through Ronnie's poorly secured bun but fixing her hair would have to wait.

A couple of miles down the road, the ranch came into view at the crest of a hill. Ronnie saw the main house and several cars parked outside. It was the biggest building with several smaller ones scattered around the property. Some looked like sheds or barns, and some like the small cabins she recognized from her first night in town.

Hundreds of rolling acres surrounded these outbuildings, most of the pastures empty now except the one used for horses.

Slowing down, Colten called over his shoulder, "We've moved the cattle for the summer, but during the winter and spring months, they stay closer."

They parked near a cluster of trucks. Ronnie felt reluctant, losing the warmth of Colten's body, when she finally let go and pushed off the four-wheeler.

The main house was a single story with a covered porch along its front. Several chairs, mostly rockers, sat along the porch. "We'll be eating with the crew," Colten warned her. "They can be a rowdy bunch. But Aunt Violet promised to keep them in line."

Inside, a long table spanned the room right off the kitchen. There had to be at least ten men crowded around it. One she recognized, Jed. He looked much better compared to what Colten described yesterday. A few of the men looked up and nodded, then went back to eating. Jed waved.

"You must be Ronnie Ross," a cheerful woman with her hair tied in a gentle bun said. Aunt Violet, in an apron wrapped around her waist, welcomed Ronnie with a hug. "I'm Violet. Colten's told us so much about you."

"He has?" Ronnie let her worried gaze travel to

Colten, but he'd already taken a seat, falling into conversation with a man next to him.

"All good things, I assure you."

"I find that hard to believe."

Violet laughed at that. "And Colten thinks he's not easy to figure out. Please, have a seat. I made strawberry stuffed French toast today, and I saved some for the four of you. These men devour anything I put on the table."

"Thank you, Violet. That was very sweet of you."

Ronnie fell into the empty chair beside Colten. Reese, after her own hellos, edged her way around to sit next to Hudson. Ronnie raised an eyebrow at her friend, sitting so close to her brother, falling so easily into conversation with him. But when Violet served them all heaping plates of the most delicious-looking breakfast Ronnie'd seen in weeks, her attention diverted to the meal. At the first bite, she closed her eyes to savor the taste. "This is amazing, Violet!"

"Thank you, dear." After setting a filled pot of coffee on each end of the table, Violet finally took a seat with the other women. Several of the men were scooting from their chairs, prepared to get to work. Most of those who remained emptied the coffee pot almost immediately.

"I hear you ladies are from Chicago," Violet said, her eyes eager. "Please, tell me all about my favorite city. I haven't been back there in over a decade."

Ronnie mentioned some of the great shopping spots on Michigan Avenue, but when Reese interjected, she let her take over the conversation. Between the food, the sights, and the shopping, her friend spoke of Chicago as if it were the greatest place to live.

For years, Ronnie'd thought the same. Now, she wasn't so sure. There were certainly things she loved, like deep-dish pizza that could make your toes curl in delight. But having spent so much time in Starlight, she imagined the city would have an entirely different feel to it when she got back.

Colten was engrossed in conversation with the man Ronnie assumed was Uncle Joe, based on his age and the way he and Violet kept slipping looks at each other.

Ronnie was sure Colten didn't notice when their legs bumped each other because he didn't move away. Her heart raced at the contact. This was ridiculous, how quickly her heart beat at something so insignificant Colten didn't even notice.

"I hear you're quite the designer." Violet tapped Ronnie's hand, pulling her back to the conversation and away from the distracting nature of Colten's touch.

"I've wanted to be an interior designer since I was a kid." Ronnie told her the story about her mom letting her redecorate her bedroom when she was eleven. "From that point on, anything we did to the house, my mom consulted with me first. Then my grandma was doing the same." Ronnie'd spent entire family gatherings passed from relative to another, looking at pictures and paint samples, giving her opinion.

"It's a shame you have to head back so soon." Violet refilled Ronnie's coffee cup. "I could use some help redoing my family room. It's more outdated than Joe's haircut."

"Ain't nothing wrong with my hair." Joe scooped his hand at it, then hid it beneath a ball cap.

"Sure, honey."

"I might be able to take a look sometime next week?" Ronnie offered. She didn't have a set date to leave. It wasn't as though she had anywhere lined up to live. Going back to Chicago now meant she had to move in with her parents until she lined up a place. But she didn't know how long Becca would let her stay, either. Even if they took the day off tomorrow, which Colten was insisting they do, they'd finish by Tuesday. Becca was due home on Wednesday.

"I'd love that!" Violet tapped Ronnie's hand again, a friendly gesture it seemed. "Thank you, dear."

"Of course. Happy to help."

Ronnie polished off her French toast, stuffed at the last bite.

"Most amazing breakfast, Violet!" Reese's chipper voice shook Ronnie from the looming food coma. "Do you cater to project sites? I'd pay good money!"

Violet laughed. "No time. These boys keep me in the kitchen most of the day. They've got ravenous appetites." She carried empty plates to the island counter in the kitchen, and once they were all cleared, asked, "Colten, you boys taking these pretty ladies to The Watering Hole tonight? There's live music out on the deck."

"Well—"

"How about it?" Hudson asked, cutting off Colten. "I could use a relaxing evening with some music and dancing. You girls in?" He ignored his hesitant best friend.

"Absolutely!" Reese chimed in, then instantly looked at Ronnie. "If we'll have time?"

All eyes fell on Ronnie. Did they think she was some workaholic who insisted everyone slave away while the rest of the town had a good time on a Saturday night? "The floor shouldn't take too long. That's all I have on my to-do list today. If we all tackle it, I think live music sounds fun."

"I would," Colten said, "But you'll have to go without me. Uncle Joe needs some help—"

"Pish-posh," Violet jumped in. "Joe'll get your help this morning and into early afternoon I suspect, but the rest will have to wait."

"But—"

"Colten James Livingston, if you expect to keep

eating my cooking, you'll go out with these fine young ladies tonight and make sure they have fun."

"Yes, ma'am."

Ronnie wanted to be excited about the prospect of a fun night out, especially with her only friend visiting. But Colten seemed eager to be anywhere else but out with her.

CHAPTER 17

onnie

THIS WAS GOING TO SUCK. No way around it. But she'd finally tracked Hudson down at his cabin. He looked worn, as if he'd worked hard. Harder than usual. Perhaps he wanted to make sure enough was done at the ranch in time to go out tonight.

"Hey," she said. "Got a minute for your little sister?" Her voice felt tiny. It didn't help how much her brother towered over her.

Hudson tossed his hat into the lone chair on his small deck. "Sure." He reached for the doorknob, but then reconsidered. "I stink. Probably best not to confine us both to a small cabin with weak air conditioning."

"Yeah, good call."

Hudson dropped onto the top step and patted a spot next to him. "What's on your mind?"

Ronnie'd spent countless hours deciding how to best approach the news, but none of the variations sounded right. "I got fired."

"Becca fired you?"

"No. Lana. A couple weeks ago."

"But—"

"That's why I suddenly had two weeks' vacation." Her steady voice began to tremble, no matter how much she tried to stay strong. "I was late for a really important project and she didn't care why. She fired me in front of everyone. I'm sure it'll be on the show in a week or two."

"Why didn't you tell me?" Hudson's low voice was hard to hear through the whipping wind that whirled up.

"I was embarrassed. Couldn't stand the thought of how humiliated I'd be . . . telling you." The first tear fought its way to freedom. "I tried to tell you the first night I was in town, but—"

"I invited friends to dinner. Didn't give you a chance."

"I didn't mean to land a job. But once I did, I didn't know how to make it right without embarrassing you. I thought if I could pull this off, Lana would hire me back and no one would have to know the difference. You wouldn't have to . . ."

Hudson put his arm over her shoulder and pulled her against him. Ronnie didn't even mind the ranch smell. At least Hudson wasn't storming off as she'd feared. "I'm sorry, Ronnie. It's my fault for putting you in that position. I thought that job was what you wanted. That you liked working for Lana Bojanski. I couldn't really see why, but that didn't matter. It was your dream, not mine."

Tears of relief fell now. "I thought you'd be disappointed in me."

"Never." He roughed up her hair as he pulled his arm away.

"Hey!"

"You're family. I'm not allowed to be anything but supportive."

"Gee, don't I feel special."

"I'd never be disappointed in you for the wrong reasons, Ronnie. You worked so hard for a promotion. One that was taken away from you. Last night when I was helping Reese with that dining room fixture, she told me all the hours you worked. How Lana'd call you in the middle of the night. How did you sleep?"

Ronnie sputtered a laugh. "I didn't some nights."

"That's no way to live."

"That's why I'm not going back."

"To Chicago?"

"To Lana." Ronnie took a deep breath. "I thought I wanted my job back, but now I don't think any offer would be worth what I put up with. I'm not sure what I'm going to do, or where I'm going to live when I go back, but I'll figure something out."

He hugged her again, holding on tighter than before. "You're one of the strongest people I know, Ronnie. You'll land on your feet, no matter what you decide."

"Okay, you need a shower. We only have an hour to get ready."

He hopped to his feet, a smile forming that lit up his eyes. "You're right."

"Hudson, are you—"

"Hurry up and get ready," he interrupted. "You have a smudge of paint on your cheek, by the way."

RONNIE SCRUBBED AT THE PAINT. She'd only spent five minutes with an edging brush and still managed to splatter some on her face. Figured. The last remnants were stubborn, but she refused to be seen in public looking like she was wearing war paint.

"I bet your cowboy would help you get that paint off," Reese teased, camped out there at the small sitting desk in the bedroom Ronnie'd commandeered, her folding mirror propped open as she fixed her makeup. Though Becca had told Ronnie not to worry about a thing on the upper level, Ronnie would love to redo that bathroom. The lighting was dim and the counter space nonexistent. Maybe knocking out a wall and expanding it into a walk-in closet for the bedroom would work. However, that wasn't only outside of Becca's budget, it was certainly outside the timeline and Ronnie's skillset.

She poked her head around the corner, admonishing Reese. "Don't go getting any crazy ideas, okay? He's Hudson's best friend."

"So?"

"That makes him off limits by default."

Reese cackled a laugh. "You keep using that lame excuse. I think Hudson would be pretty happy to see you two together."

"Reese, you know I'm not staying, right?"

"There's no rule says you can't kiss him just because you're not staying. That'd be a perfect waste of a good cowboy." Her friend stepped into the vanity mirror beside Ronnie, only half her bronze eye shadow applied. Reese waved her makeup brush around as she spoke. "But have you *really* decided you're not staying?"

"How could I possibly stay?" Ronnie hoped her tone dismissed this topic once and for all. "Once this project's done, I've got nowhere to live."

"You have the same problem in Chicago."

"If you're so interested in this idea, why don't you go after him?"

Reese giggled all the way back to her sitting desk and dropped onto the creaky chair. "Honey, that man only has eyes for you. Even *if* I wanted him, I wouldn't stand a chance."

"That's not true," Ronnie fired back. Just because they'd shared an explosive kiss in the moonlight didn't mean Colten had any sort of interest. He was the one who called it a mistake. He was the one who hadn't even reacted to their legs touching all the way through breakfast.

"You're blushing."

Ronnie jumped, expecting her friend to be standing beside her again. But Reese sat at the table, applying mascara. "Am not."

"Knew it!" Reese packed up her makeup in a silver travel case and zipped it shut. "With the electric tension between you two, you could rival a lightning show. You should have seen him light up at the sight of you when he came back today to help with the floor."

Ronnie had to admit when Colten's truck pulled up, it had felt as if he was coming home. It was a ridiculous fantasy, to think of him coming home from a long day on his family's ranch. Coming home to her. In a house that his mom would put on the market within days of returning from Denver.

"Spill it."

"What?"

Reese's eyes narrowed, intensely staring Ronnie down. But Ronnie held firm. "I don't know what you're talking about."

"Something happened."

"Nothing happened." But the lie consumed her. Would it be so bad to share her secret with one other person? Telling her only close friend didn't mean that Hudson ever had to find out. "There's nothing to tell."

"I don't believe you." Reese hovered like a hawk. "You *kissed* him, didn't you?"

"What?" Ronnie's face was surely a deeper red than her shirt. "I-I—"

"Ha! I knew it!"

"You can't say anything, Reese!"

"Fine, but—" A pounding on the bedroom door saved Ronnie the decision. "Crap, is it already eight?"

"No," Reese said. "We have fifteen minutes. Keep working at that cheek. Paint's almost gone, but you'll need some foundation to cover up the red spot you created."

The knocking sounded again. "Probably Hudson. Go!" Ronnie shooed her friend. "Distract him."

Reese skittered away. "Coming!"

A sigh of relief left Ronnie when the door closed. She loved Reese. The woman was the closest friend she'd ever had. The only friend. Her long hours dedicated to her job had caused some friendships to wither away and made it nearly impossible to forge new ones. But Reese never seemed to mind Ronnie's workaholic lifestyle.

But now Ronnie wondered how many things she'd missed out on because of her choices. Would she have more girlfriends? Would she have a relationship? Would she work somewhere she loved?

She shoved the questions aside, determined for once to let all her worries wait. Let her job wait until the morning. Tonight, she wanted a chance to relax. Enjoy some good food and live music. She'd have to keep her distance from Colten, but that shouldn't be too hard in a crowded setting. Considering how thrilled he didn't seem about going tonight, it shouldn't be too much of a problem.

THE WATERING HOLE seemed to be Starlight's main attraction on a Saturday night. A crowd of people hovered outside the door, clearly waiting for a table. An outdoor speaker, probably set up on the deck, played country music.

"We can go in," Hudson said. "I called in earlier. We have a table on the deck."

"How—" Colten started to say but stopped.

Ronnie wondered if The Watering Hole took reservations on Saturday nights. But if her brother made the call, it was no surprise. Starlight adored him. It made her happy to think Hudson had found a town who loved him as much as he loved it.

She'd been so distracted looking around at the cedar-paneled walls decked out in antique metal business signs and horseshoes that when Colten took her hand to lead her through the crowd to the deck, Ronnie had no chance to prepare. Would his touch always make her nerves tingle like this?

They sat at a table three rows back from the stage. Not too close, but enough to enjoy the band without having to yell at each other while interim music played. A sign on the stage let them know it'd be an hour before the band started. A handful of couples danced to the country music playing in the meantime.

"Aunt Violet's really disappointed you won't be around long enough to redo her family room," Hudson said to Ronnie after the waiter promised some ice water and a round of drinks. With how crowded the deck was, it seemed likely to take a while. "Sure you can't stick around a few more days?"

Ronnie struggled answering. "I wish—"

"I love this song!" Reese piped up, nudging Hudson with her shoulder. "Hudson, please tell me you don't have two left feet."

Hudson's eyes lit up at the challenge. "I most certainly do not."

Temporary relief came over Ronnie as her friend

pulled Hudson onto the dance floor. She'd told Hudson the truth, but what if he made it his mission to convince her to stay? Would she disappoint him by leaving?

"Does your city friend there even listen to country music?" Colten asked now that they were alone.

"Nope." Ronnie watched them on the dance floor, smiles wide. They danced a little closer than the rest of the couples. Odd. "Not even a little."

"What are you going to do, Ronnie?"

She ran her hands over each other trying to clear her head. "I-I don't know."

Colten placed a hand over both of hers. "Lana Bojanski isn't your only option, you know."

"In Chicago, she is."

"I don't know much about interior design, but you have a gift. Look what you've managed to pull off."

"Not on my own, though."

The waiter dropped off drinks and the appetizer Hudson had ordered for the group. But food didn't appeal to Ronnie right now. Her stomach was in knots. Colten nudged her shoulder, leaning in close to her ear. "Check out your brother and Reese." His breath against her neck sent shivers throughout her. "They're having a blast. Any chance . . ."

"Reese loves Chicago more than anyone I know." As wonderful as it was seeing Hudson having a good time, it would be temporary. He belonged in Starlight. She'd seen it everywhere she turned. "Hudson's home is here."

At the conclusion of the song, Hudson and Reese returned to the table. "Ronnie, I just learned how to two-step! It's so much fun." She dug a cheesy fry out of the basket and plopped into her seat. "I can't believe I've been missing out all these years."

"You're a quick study."

Colten batted Ronnie's leg under the table, his eyes suggesting he was still onto something when it came to those two. But that was just a reminder that once the vacation was over for her and Reese, they'd both go back to reality. Their cowboys would stay here.

The clanging of a cymbal drew their attention to the stage, where the band was setting up. "These guys are great," Hudson told the table. "They'll have the whole place on their feet within an hour."

Ronnie wasn't one for dancing, so she felt content to sit and enjoy the refreshing breeze off the river while the rest of the patrons crowded the dance floor. During the band's first song she closed her eyes and let the music disconnect her from reality. Before that kiss, fantasies of returning to Chicago and Lana begging her to take her old job back for double the pay had ruled her days. But now . . .

"Could you see yourself staying?" Colten's question was spoken against her ear between songs.

When her eyes fluttered open, she realized her brother and Reese had returned to the crowded floor, dancing a little closer than before. Colten's chair was scooted closer than it had been before the start of the first song.

"I want to say yes," she admitted.

"Then why don't you?"

The urge to slip her hands into his overwhelmed her. She couldn't quit staring at his strong hand resting so casually on the arm of his chair. But this feeling wasn't real. Was it? "What if I'm just running away from my problems?"

"You mean like your brother did?"

"That's different—"

"Not really," Colten interrupted. "But look how much good Starlight did him. He's happy. Ronnie, Hudson's like this all the time now. When he moved here, he was moody, quiet. But over time, this town healed him."

Ronnie couldn't deny the change. The few days after the wedding that never happened, she'd tried consoling him. Hudson hardly spoke a word to anyone. For weeks, she got barely more than a one-line text. But over time, he started calling. Life returned to his voice.

"What's holding you back?"

Ronnie couldn't tell Colten her greatest fears. What if the only reason she wanted to stay was to be with him? What if she decided to stay only to find he didn't feel the same? Would there be enough here for her without him? "I—"

"Colten Livingston, as I live and breathe!"

Ronnie's mouth was left agape as she took in the gorgeous woman standing at the edge of their table. Her poofy blonde hair and meticulously applied makeup were dramatic but perfect. Her strapless, glittery top accentuated an hourglass shape as if it had been custom-made for her.

Ronnie felt the bottom of her stomach drop out. She'd never seen a picture, but she didn't need one judging by the look on Colten's face.

"Danica," he said slowly. "What're you doing here?"

CHAPTER 18

Colten

Colten couldn't believe his eyes. Since the day he watched the dust trail follow Danica out of town for the last time, he'd have bet his entire life savings she'd never step foot in Starlight again. But here she was, in the flesh, dolled up like an actress.

"Is that any ol' way to greet your wife?"

Colten tensed, knowing full well what she was doing. Would Ronnie hold this against him? He'd been pretty tight-lipped about his past. With Danica's little show, it certainly wouldn't help paint an accurate picture. "Ex," he reminded her, his voice loud enough to break through the noise behind them. "Ex-wife, Danica."

"Well, details." Her long blonde hair bounced with her giggle, something he used to find irresistible about her. But now, it was just irritating.

Ronnie's smooth fingers slipped into his hand, interlocking with his own. She didn't owe him this favor but offered it anyway. His heart pounded at the contact. He wasn't sure if that was from Ronnie's touch or a fear that Hudson would see them holding hands and make assumptions he wouldn't be too pleased about.

Hudson had arrived hardly two weeks after Danica disappeared. They'd never met.

"What brings you to town, Danica?" Colten tried to solve the puzzle. "I thought you hated this place." He couldn't imagine a single thing that would entice her to return to the place she so clearly despised. Danica didn't have any family here, and she hadn't exactly made friends during her brief period as a resident. In fact, she made quite a few enemies.

"I heard you're leaving. Had to come see that for myself."

Colten tensed, wondering how on Earth she'd heard anything. The only person he shared that tidbit with was his mom, and she didn't even care for Danica when he was married to her.

"Leaving?" Ronnie repeated, her voice quiet so Danica wouldn't hear.

He squeezed her hand, hoping she knew it

meant he'd tell her everything first chance he got. "You might want to check your sources."

"I heard your mother made an offer on a house in Denver."

That, Colten could believe, was news that might spread around town. But he was still confused about who Danica had kept in touch with. Probably some cousin in Denver she'd bumped into.

"Yes, my mom *is* moving. But I haven't made any plans. Starlight's my home. A home you sped away from so fast the dust trail rose a mile high in the sky."

Danica tossed her hair over her shoulder. More than one guy had his eyes on her performance. Colten wished one of them would come steal her away. More than anything, he wished he could slip out and go home. Anywhere she went, Danica's big personality never left much room for anyone else. "It's true, I had some trouble . . . adjusting."

"That's one way to put it." The bitterness seeped out of him. Being abandoned while going through one of the hardest times in his life could do that to a guy.

"This the designer?" Danica nodded toward Ronnie as though she were a prop, not a person. "The famous one from TV?"

"Yes," was all he'd say through gritted teeth. Colten stroked Ronnie's hand with his thumb, hoping she knew how terribly sorry he was she had to sit here through this disastrous reunion.

"That house was so terribly outdated. I can't wait to see how it looks brought up to the twenty-first century." Unless they were bringing in granite countertops, commercial-grade appliances, and marble floors, it would never come close to something Danica would approve of. "Might have to stop by and check it out."

"Please don't," Colten said.

"I didn't catch your name, sweetheart."

"Veronica."

"From Chicago, I heard?"

How much had Danica squeezed out of the few people in this town? Colten swallowed a curse. Who'd even give her the time of day? "Can you excuse us, Danica? We're overdue for a spin on the dance floor."

"Save me a dance?" Danica batted her fake eyelashes.

"No, thanks." Colten pulled Ronnie to her feet, passing Hudson and Reese on their way back to their table, ignoring Danica's mouth, agape at what she probably considered a rude interruption.

The upbeat song ended, and a slow one started. Colten refused to drop Ronnie's hand until they were safely buried in the crowd of swaying couples. He twirled her into his arms and placed one hand on her waist. "I'm sorry you had to endure that," he whispered against her ear.

"She's . . . something."

"Yeah." In silence Colten pulled her closer, and Ronnie rested her head on his shoulder. They swayed to the slow music. At least, he hoped the music covered the pounding of his heart. With Ronnie in his arms, he could easily forget that his ex-wife was here to cause trouble. At least she didn't know anything about his call to Glacier. She was only jumping to conclusions based on his mom moving.

Sooner or later, he'd have to make up his mind should the job be offered. A few days ago, it seemed a no-brainer. But here on the dance floor, Ronnie fitting so perfectly in his embrace, Colten wasn't sure *what* his future held. With the realistic possibility that Ronnie'd leave next week, maybe tonight it was best to live in the moment. At least for this one dance.

"We could leave," she said as the song wound down. "I am a little tired."

Something inside him thawed. "Yeah?"

Ronnie should be livid Danica showed up and acted the way she did. Any other girl he knew would be pulling away from him, convinced he'd go back to her. Danica tended to have that effect. But Ronnie seemed to be saving him instead. "If we walk home, those two could take the truck."

Home. That word again, tugging at him.

"Hey, guys," Colten said to the two back at the table. "I've got a bit of a headache."

"Does that headache have a name?" Hudson nodded in Danica's direction, then reached for more of the cheesy fries. Danica was posing, leaned up against the bar, flirting with someone next to her, probably earning herself a free drink. Yeah, he definitely didn't need to be here once she had a couple of drinks in her.

"Sure does."

"Would you be upset if we took off?" Colten didn't realize until that moment that their fingers were still interlocked.

Ronnie leaned against his arm, her other hand touching his bicep. "We're hoping *someone* will take the hint not to chase after him."

"Oh!" Reese nodded. "Do you want us to come back with you?"

"No," Ronnie said, shaking her head. "Stay, enjoy the music. She doesn't know who either of you are. No reason to let her spoil your evening."

"I can drop you off," Hudson jumped in. Colten's shoulders tensed, wondering if there was anything accusatory in his offer.

"You two seem to be having a good time," Ronnie replied. "Stay."

It did appear as if Hudson and Reese were hitting it off, if their chairs scooted together and shared glances were any indication.

They worked out the details, Colten agreeing to leave the truck for Hudson and Reese. Though

Ronnie wore her wedge sandals, she'd tossed a pair of flats into the truck in case her feet started to ache. The walk back to the house was almost two miles, but Ronnie didn't mind—as long as Danica didn't follow them.

"Doubt she'd get far in stilettos," Ronnie teased.

"Right." Colten almost lost his composure at the thought of another moonlit walk alone with Ronnie. At least they'd be showered in streetlights most of the way. That should keep him out of trouble.

When they were two blocks from The Watering Hole and the echo of music faded, Ronnie asked, "Can I ask something without offending you?"

Colten laughed at that. "I don't know how I'm supposed to respond to that question."

"How'd you end up marrying Danica?"

Shoving his hands in his pockets, an amused smile fell across his face. "Sometimes I ask myself the same thing." He shook his head, hoping to ward off more, but Ronnie kept looking at him, waiting for an answer as they continued down Main Street. "I met her in Denver. Different time. We were younger." He shrugged. "Danica was different then, too. More down-to-earth. And she had an ambition about her, like I had about myself. You know, that whole desire to make waves. She actually liked Starlight the few times we visited."

"She seemed pretty comfortable tonight."

"Oh, she always is for the first few days." Colten

knew what would happen. Danica would shove her way in his path as much as she could, talking endlessly about how much she missed this place. How much she wanted to come back. "But within a week, she'll be ready to sprint as far away as she can. This town isn't big enough for her." Colten thought it only fair to warn Ronnie that his ex would most likely show up at the house tomorrow as if she owned the place. "She never liked it there."

"She seems more the modern contemporary type."

"I'll pretend I know what that means." The air between them was light again, and for that Colten was grateful.

He'd dropped her hand once she changed her shoes back at the truck, and it seemed silly to reach for it again as if Danica might be lurking in the shadows to see whether they were really a couple. But now he reached out and squeezed her hand. "Thank you."

"For what?"

"For getting me away." He glanced back over his shoulder even though The Watering Hole was out of sight. "Are you sure you don't want to go back?"

"Nah." He felt her whole body shiver through her hand. She had to be cold in her thin, flowing cotton shirt. Those tiny sleeves were hardly sleeves at all. In all the commotion with Danica, Colten hadn't noticed how lovely the dark red color looked on her. He almost told her so, but where would that leave them?

He shrugged out of the jacket he'd grabbed from his truck and draped it over her arms. "I'm burning up, and you were not properly dressed to walk home in a cool summer breeze."

She tried to argue at first, but finally just said, "Well, thank you then."

Silence stretched as the blocks disappeared behind them, giving way to downtown and residential areas. Colten had always loved this walk. The urge to leave, to spend his days roaming countless acres of wilderness seemed less exciting with Ronnie beside him. Maybe all he'd needed was a reason to stay in Starlight.

"You think you could ever live in a place like this?" Colten dared to ask. "I mean *really* live here. Even when it's five degrees with a foot of snow and wind gusts that chill you right to the bone?"

She stopped near the corner of the street, just shy of the orange glow of the streetlight, and looked around. "I don't know why you didn't go into sales. You're a natural." Her eyes found the lookout point they'd visited a few day ago, a smile forming on her lips. "If Ernie could keep enough supplies in stock to get me through a Wyoming winter, I think I could."

"Really?"

"I've always been a city girl," she admitted as they turned a corner. "I'm not used to the quiet.

And I might have to petition to get a coffee stand up and going to make it worthwhile." He watched Ronnie tilt her head toward the sky. "But these stars . . ."

"Pretty amazing, huh?"

"You can't see half this many when you drive an hour out of Chicago. Not even close."

Mom's house appeared much too quickly, and Colten found himself desperate to keep Ronnie's company. "Want to sit out on the porch with me?" he offered.

Hesitation hung in the air, Ronnie's lips parted halfway. "It's getting late."

"There're blankets inside. I'll bring you one." Colten wasn't about to give up. "Bet you didn't know that the porch has a pretty amazing view of the stars." That was the best he had. If she said no this time, he'd have to drop it.

"Okay."

Without much forethought, Colten grabbed her hand and led her onto the porch. He wasn't prepared for how the simple graze of her fingers made his heart pound. "Sit yourself down right there." He pointed to the rocker his mom frequented. He scooted his dad's next to hers and promised, "Be right back."

Lou had spread out on his bed, hogging the middle as usual. She lifted her head a moment when he came in. "You wanna sit outside, girl?" Colten asked as he scoured his closet for the softest, warmest blankets his mom had stocked.

She dropped her head back down to her paws and closed her eyes. "Sure, Lou. I know it's past your bedtime." Not much enticed her after ten-thirty. Colten gave her a quick rub and hurried back down the stairs.

It wasn't until Colten was back downstairs again and ready to step onto the porch when what was about to happen hit him. His dad's rocking chair had been empty since he passed.

"What's wrong?" Ronnie looked from him, following his gaze to the chair. She seemed to understand. "Don't you think he'd want someone to use it? Otherwise it just fades and collects dust."

Colten slipped into the chair before he could talk himself out of it, tense for only a moment. Ronnie reached her hand to his. "You okay?"

"Yeah. Actually, I am." What was happening between them? Ronnie didn't plan to stay. And he thought her show at The Watering Hole was to ward off Danica's dramatics. But they'd sure been acting like a couple since.

"This is pretty amazing," she said. "Not quite the overlook point, but a close second."

It was nights like these he'd always imagined spending with the woman he married. Nights so simple and quiet, rocking away in the silence, tucked under soft fleece blankets and the stars above.

"You really love it out here, don't you?" Ronnie finally broke the easy silence.

"More than words can say."

"It must've been hard when Danica left."

Colten swallowed a groan. They'd talked about his ex enough for one night, hadn't they? But if there was even an inkling of hope that Ronnie might decide to stay, there needed to be honesty between them. "Truthfully, it nearly broke me in two. I know she seems. . ."

"A bit over the top?" Ronnie offered.

"Yeah, that's one way to put it. She's the same in some ways, but in most ways she's a complete stranger."

"People change."

"Yeah. Even a city girl can come around to country living, right?"

Ronnie smiled, her chocolate eyes more an amber color in the glint of the moonlight. Colten could get used to that. "Right." That smile, well, it made everything else melt away for a few moments.

Dropping her hand, he reached an arm around her shoulders and allowed her head to rest on his shoulder. It was the simplest thing in the world, her head resting so easily against his chest. But it felt like the biggest thing in Colten's world right now.

"Tell me about your dad."

Colten swallowed, the familiar ache in his chest tearing at him. At first, he considered changing the subject; it would be easier than reliving the pain. But if his dad were still here, Colten would want him to meet Ronnie. "He was the best." Colten swallowed. "Actually, that's a lie. He worked too much. The ranch was everything to him. Spent more nights there than he did at home. But he did it all for us. Wanted us to have the best life. And he loved my mom." He cleared his throat, the tug of a tear coming on. "He loved to go fishing. Helped me catch my first shoe."

"Hey," Ronnie teased, nudging him.

"It's true."

"Is it hard to be here?" she asked. "In this house?"

"I thought it would be," Colten admitted. "For the first few days, I kept looking for him every time I heard a creak on the stairs. But now, the house feels different. It feels like it's getting a second chance. I think my dad would like what you're doing with the place."

She nestled into him, as close as she could with the arms of the rocking chair between them. "I'm glad."

The perfect evening. They rocked together in silence. It was foolish to wish for more than Ronnie could possibly promise. But Colten would give almost anything if she stayed, spent every summer night rocking in these chairs with him, watching the stars.

"What would it take, Ronnie?"

"For what?"

"To convince you to stay?" He felt her turn and met her gaze. It was impossible not to kiss her. He'd been fighting the urge for too long. The harder he fought, the worse the desire grew.

Her soft hand cupped his cheek. "You know I can't promise anything." Her voice was a soft whisper. "I don't know what I'm going to do yet."

"Then promise me what you can." Hopefully he could show her plenty of reasons to stay before their time was up. "Even if it's only a few days."

"Okay."

His lips met hers, and he savored the sweet kiss. There was no longer any fight in him to keep from falling for Ronnie Ross. This cowboy had fallen too far to turn back.

CHAPTER 19

onnie

WITH A YAWN THE NEXT MORNING, Ronnie asked, "You want to do *what*?"

"Take out the wall." Colten stood in the doorway to the kitchen, sledgehammer in hand. "I had an engineer come by an hour ago. He confirmed it's not loadbearing. Let's take it down."

"But I just painted that wall!" Ronnie couldn't believe where this was going. They'd nearly finished the renovations. Becca would be back in a couple of days, and Ronnie'd hoped to coast through the final minor touches still on her punch list. "I have to run to Gillette today, and . . . Where on Earth did you round up an engineer so last minute?"

"Thank your brother. This town loves Hudson. And sorry, but yeah. We'll have to repaint what's left."

"I think it's a great idea!" Reese chirped from behind Colten, scribbling into a notebook at the kitchen counter. "Think of how open and inviting this space will be!"

She thought on it. Squinted, and stepped back a pace. Of course they were right. Even with the upper portion of the wall down, the space would open up considerably. But Ronnie couldn't imagine why Colten suddenly thought he needed to destroy a whole wall.

"I think it's a good idea, too," Hudson confirmed, popping in from the kitchen. Ronnie wasn't sure whether he'd been in there drinking coffee or had somehow snuck in from the deck door. "More family friendly that way."

"And," Reese said to Colten, "I have to go to Gillette anyway. I checked with Ernie, but he doesn't have the backsplash we want." Reese winked. "Hudson offered to come with me to pick it up. They have it there. Ronnie, you can just send your list with me." The twinkle in Reese's eye suggested she was doing Ronnie a favor behind running errands.

"Backsplash?" Ronnie chimed in.

"For the kitchen," Colten answered, as though there was no surprise to his words.

Ronnie patted a finger at her own chest. "And

who was planning to tell the designer that you added another room to your renovation plans?" Ronnie hadn't gotten enough sleep to process what was happening. She'd been awake half the night thinking of those kisses. "The only kitchen project I knew about was the floor, and that's done."

"Sorry," Reese said. "We only decided an hour ago. But it's just backsplash. For the south wall behind the sink."

"How did you get Ernie—" Ronnie shook her head. Even though the hardware store was closed on Sundays, she'd little doubt one of the two men in the room had finagled something. But without her morning cup of coffee she wasn't about to put too much thought into what was already done.

Ronnie softened at the sheepish look on Reese's face, not missing the quick glances and smiles she kept exchanging with Hudson. What transpired at The Watering Hole after she and Colten left? "If it's only backsplash . . ." Ronnie shooed them away with her hand. "My list is in the other room. Please don't take all day. With any luck, we can get most of the house finished today. Well, maybe the kitchen tomorrow."

"So, how about it?" Colten asked, nodding at the wall he wanted to take down.

Ronnie shook her head, in disbelief that everyone had made plans without her. She brushed past Colten to get into the kitchen, amazed how the lightest touch of skin could still unravel her. "You know we'll have to take down these upper cupboards first." At least there weren't any major appliances on this wall other than the fridge. "Let's leave the fridge in the corner though, okay? We don't need to demolish the whole wall."

"Are we saving the cupboards?" Reese asked.

Ronnie scanned the kitchen. If there was one thing this kitchen had plenty of, it was cupboard space. "No. But the dumpster's gone."

"I can haul them," Hudson volunteered. "Leave them on the porch and I'll pick them up when we get back from Gillette."

"I think we should do a pony wall, only take down the upper half. Do a passthrough, a wider window space." Ronnie and Colten went back and forth on the design plans, her hands up, drawing in the air, fashioning what they'd end up with. She finally convinced him to leave the counterspace and lower cupboards. "It'll still give that open feeling," Ronnie promised. "And if you don't like it, we can take down the rest."

"We'll be back!" Reese skittered out the door, Hudson close behind.

Ronnie studied the wall. She'd watched countless crew members do this before and knew the first step was to take a utility knife and cut into it to find the electrical wires. "Do you have a buddy who's an electrician?" she asked before she was willing to make the first cut.

"Yep. Pete will be by in an hour."

"Of course," Ronnie mumbled. It had taken her two years to cement solid relationships with contractors and retailers in Chicago, but Colten's friends *came by* with just a phone call.

"Small town living, darlin'." Colten winked at her. "Goes a long way around here."

"But you don't even have options."

"Sure there are," Colten countered. "There're three electricians in Starlight. But Pete's the only one worth his weight in gold. No one else would even entertain stopping by on a Sunday." Colten picked up the sledgehammer, leaning on its handle. "One guy's slower than molasses in a snowstorm. The third doesn't call anyone back unless you're willing to pay him upfront. But Pete, if you need him, he'll show up in the middle of the night."

What would it be like to live in this town, Ronnie wondered. To know those people in much the same way she knew the ones in Chicago? In Starlight, people did favors without expectation of anything in return. People cared about more than making a profit.

"Guess we can tear out cupboards while we wait for Pete," Ronnie finally suggested. She turned toward the kitchen doorway, but a hand reached for hers and spun her around.

Colten's hand slid along her neck. "I've been wanting to do this since last night." He drew her lips to his. Tingles shot down through her toes at those soft, warm lips. When he let her go, Ronnie fell against the doorframe, her legs limp as noodles. She couldn't quite catch her breath.

Colten winked at her again, then reached for the sledgehammer propped against the kitchen table. "You wanna take the first swing?"

Ronnie wasn't sure how they managed to take down the cupboards and the upper portion of the wall, considering her mind stayed in a dizzy spin of emotions. She wanted to believe something was blooming between them, but it seemed dangerous to let herself get carried away.

"I think we have everything on your list," Reese, back from Gillette, said to her. "Earth to Ronnie?"

"Sorry. Thank you." Ronnie had taken the opportunity to slip outside to help unload everything from Hudson's truck. She desperately needed the fresh air. Leaning against the truck, she asked, "Did you have trouble finding any of it?"

"Nope." Reese wore a smirk that unsettled Ronnie.

"What?"

"Oh, you know what." Reese waited until both

Hudson and Colten were inside before she added, "You and that cowboy, that's what."

"Um—"

"Ha! I knew it."

"Please don't say anything yet." She and Colten were still trying to figure out what to say to her brother. They'd gone back and forth all morning about whether to tell Hudson or wait until Ronnie knew what she was going to do. What would be the point if she ended up leaving?

"You decide yet? About staying?" Reese asked.

"No," Ronnie admitted, pushing off the truck and reaching for a box. "And that's the problem. I don't know what I'm going to do."

CHAPTER 20

olten

BEYOND UPDATING THE FLOORING, Colten never intended to let Ronnie's renovation project touch the kitchen. Sure, looking at it though her eyes, it *was* a little outdated. But overall, the room was in good shape. Perfectly functional for selling.

But last night, he decided he'd do whatever he could to convince her to stay. Prolonging the renovation project bought him an extra day he needed to pull off a few miracles. If only there were time, he'd have them redoing the whole house. But between his mom coming back in two days and the clock ticking for Ronnie's departure back to Chicago, options were limited.

"Would you look at this?" A recognizable whistle sent bristles through Colten, and his entire demeanor tensed. Thankfully Ronnie and Reese had taken Lou for a walk to the stream. He wanted to give her the space to think through her options.

"Danica, what are you doing here?" He expected she'd make at least one appearance before she left town for another two years. Hopefully longer. He had no reason to smile. Dealing with Danica wouldn't do Ronnie any good.

"I heard Becca was renovating, but I had no idea." Danica stalked the room like a lioness on the prowl, each click of her stilettos deliberate. "This floor, it's so elegant. Feels a little masculine in here though with those gray walls. Needs a woman's touch, don't you think?"

It was no surprise that Danica was all dolled up, missing the sparkly top from last night but still in the full hair and makeup getup. How had he ever fallen for her?

He had to admit that Ronnie in her wild, messy bun and barely-there makeup looked so much more enticing.

"Are you on the lookout to buy a house in Starlight?" His question was intended as a jab, but suddenly, facing her, he feared she might say she was.

"You know I'm not a fan of having a mortgage." She slithered her fingers along the cedar trim lining the bay window. "Too restraining. But if you know of any apartments coming up, be sure to let me know."

He remembered all too well. Danica wasn't one for setting roots in anywhere. "Maybe you should get a paper. Check the want ads," he said, trying to usher her toward the front door but she failed to take the hint.

"Good ol' Starlight and its ancient newspaper. Can't believe that thing still prints. 'Course, folks don't really know how to function without it around here, do they?"

"Come back another time? Like, two years from now?" It was a low jab of his own, but he couldn't help it. He'd confessed the truth to Ronnie about Danica last night, but he didn't trust his ex not to cause trouble.

She batted her eyelashes and gave him her best pouty face. "You missed my performance last night. I sang with the band." It may have worked on many other men, but it wouldn't on him. "You left with *her*."

"And?" For the first time since she came back, Danica was speechless. Had she expected him to deny it?

"She mean something to you?"

The memory of rocking on the front porch with her in his arms last night made him smile. "She does." His conviction surprised him, but he knew when it came to Ronnie Ross, he truly was a lost cause.

"You tell that girl you applied for your old job?"

The question snapped him back. "Who told you?"

"You did." A victorious, snakelike smirk curled on her lips. "Just now."

It wasn't as if they'd called with an offer, but even if they did, Colten decided he'd decline. He had his turn. It was time to let another ranger have his rotation. He was ready to plant some roots, even at the expense of the most amazing national park he'd ever worked for. "I'm not going."

That stopped her dead. Danica headed for the door. "Hope this girl is worth giving up your dream." She tossed the comment over her shoulder before she slammed her way out.

"Where are we going?" Ronnie asked, eyeing the horse with a mixture of suspicion and excitement.

"Ronnie, you have to learn to let people surprise you." Colten sat up on the front of the double saddle, then held out his hand for Ronnie to hop up behind him.

"But—"

"Let go. Enjoy the ride."

She looked back toward her friend, but Reese was

shooing her with a *Go, girl* gesture. Colten sent Reese a grateful smile for that. If it hadn't been for her help, he wasn't sure he'd have pulled any of this off.

Ronnie finally relented. "We're not done with the backsplash," she countered, but she got on the horse. "Do I at least get a hint?"

But he ignored that. Reese did, too.

"We have all day tomorrow to finish everything. Mom won't be back until Tuesday morning." He snapped the reins and Dolly moved on to take them into town.

Her persistence was adorable. Once they were protected by the cover of trees, he leaned back to plant a soft kiss on her temple. "Patience, Ronnie."

The pieces had been falling together all day, and this was only the first one. Tomorrow, he hoped it would be enough to convince her to stay. To show her that she could make a life and grow a successful business in Starlight. If Ronnie left anyway, well, then nothing would convince her to stay.

"We're really going downtown? On Dolly."

"I told you, people do that here."

Her chin rested on his shoulder. "Why haven't I seen any horses on Main Street?"

"Haven't been around long enough."

When Colten stopped Dolly near an empty storefront window, he found a confused expression on her face. "What are we doing here?"

"You'll see." After tying Dolly's reins to a nearby post, he pulled a set of keys from his pocket and jingled them toward Ronnie. "Go take a look."

"What am I supposed to be *looking at*?"

"I have a crazy idea."

"We're not redoing the upstairs bathroom." Ronnie folded her arms across her chest, a hard look in his direction. It was all Colten could do not to laugh. "We definitely don't have time for that extra project."

"No," Colten agreed. "You're right. Not today."

"No more tearing down walls."

Placing his hands on her shoulders, he met her gaze. An electrical current buzzed through him at the contact. *Would it always be this way with her?* "What if you opened your own interior design business?"

Ronnie's face changed in a second, realization gathering slowly in that confused gaze.

"You don't need some big, fancy firm to give you a career. Ronnie, what you did with that house . . . it's amazing." He brushed her cheek lightly with his knuckles. "I wanted you to know you had options, in case you decided to set up shop in Starlight." Her eyes grew with her smile. "What—"

"Go. Take a look inside," Colten encouraged as his phone buzzed in his pocket. "The details are on that desk against the far wall. See if it has any potential." Ronnie practically ran through the door in her excitement.

With any luck, this phone call would lock everything else in place. Maybe Ronnie would take his advice. Maybe, just maybe, the woman spinning around inside the empty storefront, a cheesy grin on her face, would make Colten's life complete. And stay.

CHAPTER 21

onnie

THE NEXT MORNING, Reese stopped Ronnie on the stairs, the last of her luggage in hand. "I need to show you something."

"Reese, you have to get on the road!" Her friend had a flight to catch, and at this rate she'd miss it.

She winked at Ronnie. "I can reschedule it. It's not on my dime anyway." But she didn't offer up any more details. "This is too important. Grab your coffee and let's head outside. You'll want to be sitting down."

A few birds chirped in the trees nearby, but other than Lou following them onto the porch, they were alone. Uncle Joe had called; Colten and Hudson were needed at the ranch today. It was kind of perfect, actually. Time to say thanks and good-bye. She wouldn't talk about Colten finding the storefront for her, though. That was still too iffy to discuss. Ronnie knew she'd miss her friend, especially if she decided to stay. But to also have a few hours by herself to add the finishing touches to her design was a dream come true. No chaos in the background. No contractors finishing up between camera takes.

"Please don't be mad." Reese covered her cheeks with the flats of her hands, her eyebrows drawn in worry. "I may have been hiding something from you."

"Hiding? What?"

"So, you remember when I asked to see those before pictures?" Reese had a tablet clenched in her hands "I had an ulterior motive." Her screen was held up to her chest. Reese's face squinted in what Ronnie could only describe as fear. "I promise, I had the best intentions."

Ronnie set her steaming coffee mug down. "Reese, you're starting to worry me. What is it?"

"I may have been posting an ongoing story of your project . . . online."

"What, now?"

"At first no one really paid any attention, but it sort of spread overnight. Turns out that boost feature really works." Reese breathed out, nodded, then handed her tablet to Ronnie. "I made a Facebook page for the Starlight House Project. I thought if I posted some before and after pics, added in some humorous moments . . . well, maybe a few people might comment. Share. Help you land any job you wanted in Chicago, when you came back. Even if Lana blacklisted you."

"Twenty *thousand* people liked this page?" Ronnie's eyes bugged out a bit before they refocused. Surely she'd seen that wrong. Maybe she needed glasses.

"I didn't mention the show at all. That could cause completely different issues. But people recognized you anyway." Reese hugged her knees. "People *love* you, Ronnie. You've got so many fans!"

Ronnie scrolled through the feed. The before and after progress shots were wonderful, and people ran comments for each one. But it was the cute memes that Reese created that won them over the most. "You basically made a comic strip following our project?"

Ronnie could have hugged her, but Reese's grimace was too comical. Served her right, as she apologized, "Hope you're not mad."

"Mad?" Ronnie threw her arms around Reese. "I love it! I can't believe you did this for me." Then realization dawned. "I thought you told Lana you had a stomach bug. If she sees this . . ."

"Yeah, that bug excuse was maybe a stretch,

Ronnie. I didn't want you to freak out when I told you what I really did."

"Reese?"

She shrugged, her tiny shoulders touching the tips of her ears. "When I left for my flight, I quit. Actually a few people did after Lana fired you." Reese reached for her own coffee and took a sip. "You inspired some of them to demand better. To chase their own dreams. Remember Phil?"

"The field coordinator?"

Reese leveled Ronnie with a look. "You mean the gopher guy." Phil's official title *had* only been for the show's credits. Lana ran him ragged, never happy about how long anything took. "He's been writing space operas in his spare time and decided to quit to write full-time. How wonderful is that? And then there's Angela. She was promoted to executive assistant because you left, but after a week she threw in the towel and convinced her husband to buy a plot of land to raise honey bees."

"Wow." Ronnie struggled to get air into her lungs. It was one thing to realize she'd been giving too much of herself for a boss who never appreciated her. But to know the impact this all had on the others? How long would they have put up with a job they hated if Ronnie hadn't been fired?

"If they're following their dreams, you should follow *yours*. This page, well, I think it gives you leverage to do whatever you want."

"It's crazy," Ronnie confessed. "But what if I could make it work here in Starlight? This might send clients from Gillette my way." Ronnie was doubtful a town of less than twelve-thousand people could keep her business afloat. Especially if the producers decided to air that video of her being fired. Seemed half the town would distrust her once they saw that.

Reese tapped the tablet. "What do you have to lose?"

Ronnie laughed. "My savings. Any means of leaving if I fail. Reese, what would I do here? I don't think I'm cut out to work all day on a ranch. I'm not even cut out to cook for those who do." It felt good to get that off her chest. Good to tell *someone.* She'd wanted to confess these concerns to Colten but hadn't been able to find the words. The look in his eyes, the gentle sensation of his thumb against her hand, the caress of his kiss . . . What if she let him down, too?

"Have you ever gained anything without taking some sort of risk?" Reese asked. "Your college project was a risk and it landed you that internship."

"You don't think I'd be hiding from my problems, avoiding reality out here?" Ronnie challenged.

"No. You have plenty here. Sure, your parents would miss you."

"My mom will probably think I *did* elope."

"What else are you going back to?" The words

should sting of insensitivity, but Reese was honest if nothing else. She wasn't afraid to tell it like it was. Ronnie had always admired her for that.

It wasn't as if Lana had returned Ronnie's call, and the more time she spent here, the less she wanted her to. "I really thought I wanted my job back. But I've gained some clarity out here. The way Lana treats the people who pour their heart and soul into her every request . . . I just don't get it."

"I don't doubt she'd hired you back in a heart-beat. And maybe for a couple weeks she might treat you differently. Fool you into thinking things will be better. But it'd only be a matter of time before she went back to her old ways. Is that what you want?"

"It doesn't sound so appealing anymore."

"Why *don't* you start your own business? Here," Reese said. "In Starlight. You already have your next customer lined up." When Ronnie drew in her eyebrows, Reese added, "Aunt Violet and her family room. I heard you have a possible downtown office if you want it, too."

"Of course you know about that," Ronnie said with a laugh.

"Correct me if I'm wrong, but you do have an entire storage unit filled with samples." Reese nodded toward the hill that led to the ranch. "I think you have someone who'd do just about anything to help you achieve your dream. Don't take that for granted. Guys like Colten, they're rare."

~

"Colten, you're kidding, right?" Ronnie's heart thudded. An open house? Tonight? "Your mom isn't back until tomorrow. She hasn't even seen the house."

"I sent her pictures." With his arm wrapped around her shoulder, he led her into the kitchen toward the burgers he'd picked up for lunch. "You're practically done. Couple pieces of trim, clean up the floor, and the place is ready."

"Did Becca say why *today*?" Ronnie's head spun. Colten made it sound so easy, but she'd have to dust every surface. Stage furniture. Hang curtains.

"Moving van's coming tomorrow. This is the only time to hold one while there's still furniture. You know how important that is, that real estate thing. Easier for a buyer to picture a space with some contrast."

"But the upstairs—"

"No one'll care about a little cosmetic work upstairs with how this downstairs shines." Colten slid a bottled water her way. "Mom did ask for a few things."

Ronnie played with a sweet potato fry. "Such as?"

"She wants a binder with before and after pictures. The budget. Maybe some captions on a few shots, to tell people what flooring type and stuff you used. Aunt Violet has a color printer you can use."

Ronnie didn't know how to feel. Part of her wanted to cry. She'd grown to love this house and its quirks. She put her whole heart into this project, and now it would probably have an offer by sundown. It was all happening too fast. "Wish I could buy it. Probably helps to have a steady job when asking for a mortgage though, huh?"

Colten chuckled. "Yeah, bet that doesn't hurt."

"I hope it goes to good people." Ronnie met Colten's eyes then, searching them for how he felt about all this. "This house deserves someone who will love it like your family did."

"I hope it does, too."

The afternoon zipped by in a blur, Ronnie rushing around to get every little thing perfect before people arrived. She managed to bake a couple of pans of her butterscotch brownies, hoping the scent enticed the right buyer.

"Darling, you did such a lovely job!" Violet was the first to arrive, a plate filled with finger sandwiches balanced on her hand. Ronnie scooped it from her and set it on the passthrough counter. It really did suit the openness between the kitchen and the living room. "I've known this house a long time, and this is the most alive it's ever looked. Please tell me you have time to look at my family room."

"Of course!" The possibility that Violet might be her first official client sent tingles of excitement coursing through her. It felt like a dream realized right before her eyes. "How does tomorrow afternoon work for you?"

"Once the lunch rush is through, I'm free." Violet leaned in a little closer, though they were the only two in the house. "I hear you might consider opening a business of your own here in Starlight."

"Colten's not great at keeping a secret," Ronnie said, unable to keep a small laugh from her voice. He'd certainly gone to great lengths to help this idea come to fruition. Reese was right about that. "I haven't officially decided yet, but I'm considering it, yes."

"Darling, if you do, I have a list of ladies who are eager for your services."

Ronnie smiled at the prospect, but she learned in this business never to get your hopes up until after you'd been officially hired. The list of ladies might be two friends nudged to update a room they quite loved the way it was. She'd seen it happen before.

"In fact, here's one right now! June, you have to meet this utterly talented designer. Just look at how lovely Becca's house looks."

"I recognize you from that TV show!"

Though the smile remained pasted, dread filled

Ronnie. Maybe she should call one of the producers, request some warning before that tragic episode aired. Any hope of creating a successful business in Starlight meant Ronnie needed to get ahead of that detrimental detail.

"Do you design kitchens?" June asked. "I've always wanted granite countertops."

"Kitchens, family rooms, bathrooms, bedrooms, sunrooms, you name it."

"Mine is so horribly out of date, but if I wait for Harold to get around to the updating, I'll be in my grave before it happens."

Before Ronnie could say more, Violet interjected. "Why don't you leave Ronnie your phone number? If she opens her business, she'll give you a call."

The evening flew by in much the same fashion. Several people wandered the lower floor, admiring the updates and paging through the binder she'd put together. Violet dragged folks over to introduce them to Ronnie. She'd expected Colten to add some information about the listing price, square footage, or even the lot size. But if he made a flyer, it never made it into the binder. And oddly enough, with so many here to see it all, no one asked about price.

"Where *is* Colten?" she asked Violet after the crowd trickled down to a couple of people studying the freshly tiled fireplace. Gone was the gross subway tile, replaced with a beautiful gray marble. "Haven't seen him all day."

"I'm afraid Joe kept him busy today. He wanted to be here, told me he'd try making it. But Jed's allergies acted up again. They were pretty short-handed."

"Oh, no! Is he okay?"

"Miserable, but fine." Violet appeared warmed at the concern, if her gentle smile was any indication. "Colten cares a great deal about you, you know that?"

"I—"

But their conversation was interrupted by a stylish blonde in stilettos, who pushed in. Ronnie's heart sank. "Not a terrible job." Danica sized up the living room.

"Take your shoes off. Please," Violet directed, her warm voice now going sterile and firm. "You'll scuff the floors."

Danica kicked off her heels, dropping down about four inches. She was much less intimidating at this height, but Ronnie didn't care to have her here at all. "You looking to buy a house?"

"I wonder why people keep asking me that." Danica laughed at some joke no one else understood. "No. Not quite. Just wanted to see how the final product turned out." She roamed the room, hands reaching out to feel the fabric of the curtains.

"Don't you let her bother you, darling," Violet whispered. "Danica always did love trouble."

Ronnie hoped to avoid further conversation, but when the other couple left, they were alone aside from Violet in the kitchen. About to help Violet clean up the dishes, Danica stopped her. "Heard you might be sticking around."

"I might."

"You want to reconsider that."

"Why's that, Danica?" Ronnie folded her arms across her chest, about through with this irritating woman. Every time she saw her, she witnessed the heartbreak she'd caused. Colten certainly didn't want her in town, and so far, Ronnie hadn't met anyone who did. Why was she still here?

"He put in a call for his old job at Glacier. His *dream* job. When we moved back to Starlight, his old boss promised him his spot back whenever he was ready. You stick around, you'll hold him back. He'll turn it down for sure."

"You really give me too much credit." But seeds of doubt were planted. Why hadn't he told her about that? Here she'd been struggling with her decision about Chicago, and he put in an application for his old job anyway. "Open house ended ten minutes ago. Time for you to go."

Danica grinned, slipped on her stilettos, then click-clacked her way to the door. "He deserves to live his dreams, same as you."

CHAPTER 22

olten

"WHAT ON EARTH did you *do* to my house?" Becca Livingston stood in the middle of the driveway, the door of her truck hanging open, the engine idling. "Colten James Livingston, I demand an explanation!"

Colten jogged down the drive, bracing for the lecture headed his way. Becca wasn't big on surprises, and Colten had failed to mention this extra project when they talked on the phone. "I think it looks nice."

"How do you know I even wanted it yellow?" Becca's cheeks blazed pink, but they always did when something caught her off guard. "How was there possibly enough money in the budget—"

"Side project."

"Why would you spend your own money, Colten? It's not cheap to repaint a whole house like this." The pink died down a bit, the heavy rise and fall of her chest dropping as Becca caught her breath.

Colten folded his arms around his mom and forced her into a hug. "This is for all the times you wouldn't let me do anything to the house. I know you were trying to keep me from getting wrapped up, but I've always wanted to know what it would look like yellow."

"Dad's favorite color." The smile started to form, but then it disappeared again. "What's this I hear about an open house?"

"That was more for Ronnie," Colten said, then realized he'd have to explain. "Look, you didn't get any offers."

"I haven't listed it. I better not have."

"Well, there you go." Colten slipped his arm around her shoulders. "Wait until you see the inside. You'll cool off a little bit. We'll need to discuss terms later, once you're rested up."

"For what?"

"I'm going to buy your house."

"Colten—"

"Ronnie made lunch. Hurry on up. I'll unload your bags after we eat. You'll run that fuel guzzler out of diesel if you keep it running." Colten jogged back up to the house before Becca could argue further. He knew a good home-cooked meal could help ease even the tensest of moods.

"She's mad, huh?" Ronnie asked when Colten slipped inside.

Colten just laughed. "A little. She doesn't like surprises."

"I sure hope she likes my Salisbury steak. I don't know how to make much else outside of my famous brownies."

Colten cupped his hands on her shoulders and quickly kissed her forehead. "I hope you saved some of those for dessert."

"Of course."

At the sound of his mom's boots on the porch, he pulled away. Though he wanted Ronnie to stay, Colten thought it best to keep what they had to themselves until bigger decisions had been made.

The screen door shut, and they heard, "Where's thc designer?"

Ronnie's widened eyes made him smile. She looked so cute. "She shouldn't bite," he whispered, then shoved her toward the living room.

"You took out a wall?" Becca surveyed the new gap, her eyes wide. "I don't remember mentioning taking down walls in the scope of work we discussed."

"That was me," Colten interjected. "I didn't give Ronnie a choice."

Becca's eyes left the new gap and traveled around the living room. The emotion in her eyes changed then, from irritation to something softer. "The fireplace." She covered her mouth with her hand as she kicked off her boots and moved closer to it.

"Dad always hated that subway tile," Colten said.

"He sure did." Her hands ran along the smooth marble in its place. "This is beautiful." She started to take in all the other changes. The flooring, wall color, curtains, even the trim. "This is stunning." When she turned her attention back to Ronnie and Colten, tears brimmed in her eyes. "You really did all this in two weeks?"

"I had some help," Ronnie admitted. "I mentioned my friend Reese flew in over the weekend. But Colten and Hudson were both lifesavers. Jed, too. I couldn't have done it without them."

"I'm so glad that awful carpet is gone." Becca chuckled. "That color grated on me the last couple years."

Colten saw Ronnie take a deep, steadying breath. He caught her eyes and sent her a reassuring nod. He knew what she had to do, and she'd asked him to let her make her confession on her own. "I'll set the table while you finish looking around."

Though he busied himself with plates and silverware, the aroma of lunch making his stomach growl, the passthrough window invited the conversation from the living room into the kitchen. Ronnie made her apologies and reassurances that she hadn't kept a dime of Becca's money for herself but put everything into the renovation project. "I couldn't bear the thought of embarrassing Hudson in front of people who meant so much to him."

"Does he know? About your TV show?"

"Yes." Ronnie cleared her throat. "I'll understand if you want me to leave. It was wrong to keep up the deception. I'm sorry I didn't tell you sooner, but I wanted to tell you in person."

Colten tensed as he waited for Becca to reply, to say anything. Mom could instill fear into the strongest of men. What would she do to Ronnie?

"I've never really liked that Lana Bojanski anyway."

"Mom, that's a lie," Colten hollered through the passthrough window. "You watch that show every week!"

"Doesn't matter! She's a total fake." The two women made their way into the kitchen and took a seat at the table. "If it weren't for her crew, there wouldn't even be a show. America knows darn well that Lana doesn't do much other than boss people around and take all the credit. Even Phil should get more money than *she* does."

"Phil quit." Ronnie handed the bowl of mashed potatoes to Colten, their fingers grazing. They shared a quick look, but that was enough to get his heart thumping.

"Guess I'm not surprised. Probably rattled more than a few people when she fired you."

Colten let them talk about the show throughout lunch, finding this easy interaction comforting. He couldn't remember a single meal that had gone this smoothly when it was Danica sitting opposite at the table. And she'd never had to drop such a bomb on his mom.

"Starlight could use a designer," Becca said. "Especially one so capable of actually doing the work rather than just barking orders. I think you *should* consider opening your own business. I can think of half a dozen people in town who'd hired you in a heartbeat."

"Really?" The glow in Ronnie's eyes warmed him to the core. *Could they really have a future together?*

"Told you," Colten added. His phone buzzed in the next moment, vibrating against the counter near the coffee pot. He jumped up then caught it, about to buzz right onto the floor. In a last-second catch, he kept it from shattering against the new laminate flooring.

Though he'd planned to ignore the call, the name on the screen made him freeze. Ralph. "I need to take this. If you ladies'll excuse me for a moment?"

"COLTEN, sorry it took so long to get back to you," Ralph said. "There's a whole process to these things that sucks up so much time. You remember how that goes."

"Yes, I do." Colten was waiting for a moment to interrupt, to decline the offer before Ralph gave it to him.

"Well, now that all the red tape is off, we're ready to offer you the position if you want it. An extra five grand a year from what you made last time you were here. Lot of rangers disappointed today, but I think the park is celebrating a huge win."

Colten steeled himself. "Boss, some things have come up since I put in that application. Things I can't walk away from right now." If Ronnie stayed, he'd not walk away from them at all. But even if she didn't, he was ready to put down roots. Starlight was his home. "I can't accept."

"I'm really sorry to hear that," Ralph said, "But you have forty-eight hours to make a decision. I sent over the offer letter. You look that over and then decide. We'd sure love to have you back here, so please consider it. Can you do that for me?"

"Of course." Colten stood on the porch, Lou at his feet, both of them staring out toward the rolling hill that led to the Livingston ranch. "Of course," he repeated. "Talk to you soon, Ralph. And thanks." For the past two years, working on the family ranch again made him feel as if he was merely paying his dues. But the deeper he looked into what he'd become a part of, the more he realized he loved what he was doing. Sure, some of those steers drove him crazy, and more than once he wished he could chuck his alarm through the window. But Colten loved the ranch. He loved Starlight.

His eyes fell on the kitchen window, to the table where his mom and Ronnie continued to talk as if they didn't even miss him. He loved Ronnie, too. The realization hit him like a ton of bricks to the chest. He swore he'd never fall in love with someone again, but without even trying, Ronnie Ross had stolen his heart.

"C'mon, Lou." He held the door for the dog and stepped in behind her. Tossed his phone on the counter, and it slid next to Ronnie's bigger smartphone. Hers lit up with a new message. He only meant to hand the phone over, but his eyes saw the text message anyway.

Lana Bojanski: Got ur msg. Job is urs. Call me ASAP. I need u back in town yesterday.

CHAPTER 23

 *onnie*

Ronnie pulled up to the main house of the Livingston ranch, double checking that she had everything she needed for Violet's consultation. Though she hadn't seen the room and didn't have measurements, she'd put together a handful of themes to show Violet. Piling her laptop on top of her box of samples, Ronnie headed for the door.

A part of her had hoped Colten would join her, considering this was his aunt. But when he'd returned from his call on the porch, his entire demeanor had changed. Ronnie wondered if Danica's comment had anything to do with his new mood. He'd hardly met her eyes.

Ronnie rang the doorbell.

Though the idea of staying in Starlight was certainly growing on her, she didn't want Colten to give up his dream job. Were they even serious enough for that to be a consideration? They'd known each other all of two weeks. That wasn't possibly enough time to fall—

"Ronnie, dear, come in, come in!" Violet held the door, apologizing that she'd left her on the porch with such a heavy box. Despite Violet's best attempt, Ronnie refused to let her take the heavy box from her hands. "Right this way," Violet directed her.

She led her through the dining area where they'd enjoyed breakfast yesterday, down a hall, through an arched doorway, and into a room with vaulted ceilings and a large bay window pointed toward the west.

"This has great natural light." Ronnie set her box beside the couch and had a look around. A quick assessment told her the carpet needed replacing. The walls were too dark, and the brass chandelier could use an update. But the room screamed potential. "It's a beautiful space!"

"Thank you!" Violet set a plate of fresh sugar cookies on the coffee table and motioned for Ronnie to sit. "Please, take one."

Ronnie couldn't resist a fresh cookie. "These are amazing! Are you sure you're not interested in going into business? Violet, you'd make a killing with your food."

"Maybe when I was younger. Anymore, I don't have the energy to dive into such a venture."

"That's too bad." Ronnie would pay good money to keep a plate of fresh cookies in her office for potential clients. *Her* office. The thought brought a smile to her face.

"You any closer to a decision?" Violet asked.

Ronnie swallowed, thrown that they were talking about Ronnie's future and not Violet's family room. "I'm not going back to work for Lana." That much was certain. "Chicago's a vibrant city, full of great merchants, retailers, and wonderful homes with potential. But none of it quite sizes up to Starlight."

"I'm glad to hear it."

"I brought—"

"I hope you know Colten's very dear to us. He's our nephew, but in many ways he's like our son." Violet cupped her hands around a ceramic mug. "He's been through a lot since Dave passed. Even more when you throw in Danica."

Ronnie shifted uncomfortably in her seat. Maybe this consult wasn't a consult at all. Maybe it was a warning. "I understand he gave up his dream job working at Glacier to come back."

"His dad told him not to, but Colten's stubborn. He'll do just about anything for someone he cares about. Family is everything, especially around here.

You'll figure that out come winter." Violet wore a tiny smile that hinted at more. "Hudson's become our family, too."

"I'm really glad to hear that." Ronnie's heart warmed at that. "We worried about him when he left suddenly." Ronnie wasn't sure how much Violet knew about Hudson being jilted at the altar and didn't feel it was her place to say anything. "Starlight's been good for him."

"Yes, it's been good for a lot of people. It's been good for Colten." Violet added, "You, as well."

Ronnie felt her cheeks flush. "I—"

"If you two are trying to hide it, you're doing a horrible job. It's written all over your faces lately, every time I see either one of you." Violet patted Ronnie's knee. "Just take care not to break his heart, okay?"

"Do you think I'd hold him back?" Ronnie had to know. It still bothered her—his change in demeanor after that call. Had he turned it down for her, and regretted it already? "That if I stayed he'd stay instead of going after what he really wants?"

"I think that's not something I can answer. But you know that already, don't you?" Violet set her cup on the coffee table. "Enough about all the serious stuff. Let's talk redecorating!"

~

Later that afternoon, Ronnie sped back to the house, needing to find Colten before he disappeared again. She had to know about Glacier, even if she had to pry it out of him. It had to be the reason he'd gone so solemn after lunch. No matter the cost, she wouldn't be the reason he gave up his dream.

"He took Lou fishing," Becca said from her rocking chair on the porch. "Just left a few minutes ago."

"Thanks!"

Ronnie hurried down the path, kicking off her wedges and carrying them in her hands as she ran toward the stream.

When she found him, Lou raced to her for a quick scratch behind the ears. Colten sat on the shore, tying a lure to his line.

"Hey." She wanted to jump into his arms and steal a kiss, but he didn't look particularly happy to see her.

He smiled, but it didn't reach his eyes. "Hey. Just in time to catch another shoe." But even his teasing fell flat.

"What's wrong?"

"I saw the text. From Lana."

Ronnie pulled her phone from her back pocket and scrolled through her new notifications. She'd gotten so many messages from new potential clients that they'd buried the one from Lana. "*That's* what this is about?" She leaned against him so he could see her delete it. "I'm not going back."

"But you called her."

"A few days ago, yes. But I was confused. You . . . kissed me. Called it a mistake—"

"It wasn't."

"Well, good. Lana never called me back anyway. See how little time she has for her minions? A text." She waved the phone at him. "She can't even pick up the phone to call someone."

"Well, someone is." He nodded toward her phone.

Ronnie didn't recognize the number and considered ignoring it. They needed to talk about what Colten wanted before he totally shut down the topic. But if it were a new client, she didn't want the entire town to think she was starting out impossible to reach. "Better take advantage of the bars while I have them." She hated it, but she pushed *accept*. "Hello?"

"I'm looking for Veronica Ross."

"This is she. Who's this?" She met Colten's inquisitive stare and decided to put the call on speaker. No more secrets.

"Greg Manderley," came the voice. "Executive Producer of *Design of Your Dreams*. Do you have a moment to talk?"

Her eyes widened. She couldn't imagine why an executive producer was calling her. Maybe they needed a release signed. "If you're calling to ask my permission to use the footage of Lana firing me, you're wasting your time. I'm done with that show. If my old contract doesn't cover it, you can forget it."

"Actually, we just cancelled Lana's show. We won't be airing that episode."

"What?"

"Almost everyone has quit. Not much of a show without any of the classic characters, is it? Even Phil threw in the towel." He cleared his throat. "You know how good he was for ratings." Colten smirked at that, but failed to meet her pleading eyes. What was he thinking right now? "Anyway, we realized Lana Bojanski wasn't who the viewers loved. It was everyone else. And you were the biggest hit of them all. We've been following your online story, the one about the Starlight House Project."

"Reese," she whispered to Colten.

"We'd like to talk to you about your own show. When will you be back in Chicago?"

"I—"

Colten grabbed her arm, his voice quiet. "Go."

Ronnie shook her head. She didn't want that. She'd already decided to stay here, in Starlight.

"Veronica?" Greg said when the silence deepened.

"I'm . . . not sure."

Colten refused to drop his arm, his eyes locked onto hers. "She'll be back on Monday."

"Um, great! Let's plan a meeting, say two-thirty. I'll email details."

"Oh. Okay." Ronnie felt her heart cracking open. Did Colten want her to go? All that he'd done for her, to encourage her staying, and now this pushing her away. The fantasy was shattering. A fantasy she'd been foolish enough to confuse with reality. "I'll see you then." She hung up.

"This is a big opportunity for you, Ronnie." Colten rubbed the back of his neck. "You need to go."

"I don't care about reality TV."

But his cold expression didn't soften. "This is a chance to pursue your dreams, your way. You need to do this."

Dreams.

It dawned on her. Danica's words echoed in her mind. He was pushing her away so he could chase his own dreams. If she stayed, he would too. This was the only way they could both have what they wanted. "Okay." She backed away, stumbling on a patch of rocks, but righting herself in time to turn away before Colten had a chance to see the tears streaming down her cheeks.

CHAPTER 24

Colten

"You ever gonna head home?" Jed asked.

"You sick of me already?" Colten teased, hoping to avoid answering.

A long, exhausting day at the ranch was just what Colten needed. They'd mended and reinforced a mile of barbed-wire fencing, sanded and repainted the exterior of the shed, and when they were done with that, he joined Jed in mucking out stalls. It'd kept him clear of Ronnie leaving town, kept him clear of the thoughts that twisted his insides into knots.

"Just seems a shame to waste an updated house and that big-screen TV with surround sound."

"There's no big-screen—"

"But there could be." Jed wore a cheesy smile.

"You still think I should buy the house?"

"Why not?"

Though he'd never had that conversation with his mom as he'd planned, the kid had a point. Ralph had called again, but Colten's decision to turn down the position remained firm. If he left this time, it would be to run away. Starlight was his home, and he had no reason to skip town for selfish reasons. "Maybe I will, even if it's just to keep you quiet."

"I'll still look after your horses. That truck won't pay for itself."

For the first time that day, Colten laughed. "Now I see what you're getting at." Colten put the shovel away and went to wash his hands with the garden hose just outside the stable. Jed followed. "Tell you what. Go get cleaned up, steal us some leftovers, and you can help me hook up the TV and move some furniture." His mom was having dinner with some friends as it was her last night in town. They'd talk in the morning about details. But it'd be easier to convince her to go along with things if Colten added a few of his belongings first.

"Can we watch a movie, too?"

"Sure."

"Something loud."

"What else is there?" Colten turned away from Jed, closing his eyes for a moment. He could do this.

He could go home and not see reminders of Ronnie in every detail. She'd never know how hard it'd been to watch her walk away. Every muscle in him ached to run from the stream after her; to beg her to stay.

How many designers were offered their own TV show? She deserved to hear what those producers had to say. Even if it tore him apart to let her go.

"You love her, don't you?" Jed shrugged. "Ronnie. That's the reason you told her to go."

Sometimes that kid was too perceptive for his own good. "Anyone tell you you need to quit growing up so fast?"

"Yeah." Jed smiled. "You. Yesterday."

RONNIE

Ronnie sat in the lobby of a small Chicago skyscraper, feeling sorely out of place. A month ago, she'd have been doing cartwheels off the ceiling to have such an opportunity come her way. But her mind was still in Starlight . . . even if the cowboy who'd stolen her heart no longer wanted her there to hold him back.

"Veronica Ross?" the receptionist called.

"Yes?"

"Mr. Manderley apologizes for the delay. It'll be about twenty more minutes."

"Thank you." Twenty minutes was enough time to walk ten blocks away. Reality TV had never been something Ronnie loved. Suspicions of this meeting were high, considering how hard she'd worked to stay off camera while Lana soaked up the limelight.

She pulled a notebook from her purse and began making a list—all the things she needed to get her business plan together so a bank might give her a startup loan. On the top of the open page she had written Violet's name along with details they'd discussed about the renovations.

Ugh! She'd left in such a hurry she hadn't told Violet she couldn't do the renovation of her family room. With another seventeen minutes to wait, Ronnie decided to call Starlight now before her new life took over.

"Ronnie! I was so worried about you. Hudson told us you went back to Chicago. You drove that whole way?" Violet sounded a lot like her mom, and it made Ronnie smile. Her parents would certainly be happier with her closer to them again. She'd probably have to move into the basement for a few weeks. That phone call could wait one more day.

"I'm sorry, Violet. I left a little quicker than I planned."

"You won't be able to fix up my family room, will you?"

"Not anytime soon," Ronnie admitted. She did have a storage unit full of design samples. She'd only taken a couple of boxes of essentials back with her. It would've taken too long to pack it all up. She might have changed her mind with that kind of time. "I'm sorry I waited until now to call."

"It's okay, dear. Lot of folks will be disappointed, though."

"I never should have agreed to help with that open house," Ronnie said. "I know they were there to look at buying the house, but—"

"They weren't interested in buying a house, dear. They were there to see your work. I thought you knew?"

Ronnie's pulse grew erratic. "He told me it was for potential buyers."

"Colten set the whole thing up." Violet chuckled on the other end of the line. "I think he misled you. That was all for you. Why do you think you had so many people taking your number?"

The pieces fell together, slowly. The missing listing information; the fact no one asked about the selling price. "Violet, how is he?" She braced herself for the answer. Maybe if she waited for him to leave for Glacier, she could come back to Starlight. It would be empty without him, but Hudson was still there. And the town had stolen her heart with its charm and endless number of people willing to lend a hand when needed.

"He's been mucking out stalls since you left."

"Um, oh—"

"He never mucks out stalls. That privilege is reserved for the youngest on the crew."

"I thought he'd leave."

"And go where?"

"Back to Glacier National Park."

"No, dear. He told me that doesn't hold any interest for him. He's buying Becca's house, actually." A timer dinged in the background. "Ronnie, better let you go. Got a pie in the oven. You take care now, okay?"

The phone dropped in Ronnie's lap. He hadn't left Starlight. In fact, he was putting down roots.

"Ms. Ross?" Ronnie realized the receptionist was calling out to her and looked up. From the several sets of eyes on her, it wasn't the first attempt to get her attention. "Mr. Manderley will see you now."

CHAPTER 25

olten

IT'D BEEN two weeks since Ronnie left Starlight, but she'd always be there with Colten living in this house. Colten heard almost nothing other than she'd signed a contract. He fought the urge to ask Hudson about her show.

His instincts had been right, at least.

"You're on the couch again?" Hudson filled the doorway. Had it not been for the TV, Colten might have been warned of his approach.

"It's comfortable."

"Well, get up."

"Why?"

"We need to get downtown." Hudson tossed a balled-up shirt, nailing Colten in the stomach.

"Okay, okay. No need to get violent."

Colten slipped on his boots and followed Hudson out onto the porch. "You brought horses? We gonna be in a parade?"

"Film crew insisted."

Colten tried asking, but Hudson had mounted his horse and started down the driveway. "Hurry up, Livingston," he called over his shoulder. "We're late."

"Dolly, you have any idea what's going on?" The horse nudged him in hello, but she offered no clues. Colten brought her to a canter to catch up with Hudson. They rushed through residential neighborhoods, but it wasn't until they turned that last corner that Colten saw the camera crew.

Orange cones lined either side of Main Street, blocking traffic, but Hudson trotted around them. Unsure what else to do, he followed. The crowd parted for Dolly, and it was then Colten spotted Ronnie through the lingerers. Was she holding something? Standing in front of the empty storefront, he saw she wore those wedge sandals. The words *Starlight Designs* were painted in a curly blue font on her white framed sign. Ronnie talked into the camera.

"What's going on?"

Hudson nodded forward. "Ronnie's show."

Colten's heart hammered in his chest. He'd expected her to agree to some show, to become successful and famous in Chicago. What was she doing, filming in Starlight? Maybe the producers decided to shoot some clips in the town that inspired the name of her business.

"Why are we here?" he asked Hudson, trying to keep his voice low.

"You love her, don't ya?"

Colten stared dumbfounded at his best friend, unable to form words. There'd never been an opportunity to tell Hudson before the call came in about the meeting with the producer. Not an opportunity that would have been the right one.

"You two never fooled anyone," Hudson added. "The whole town figured it out way before you did."

When Ronnie's eyes fell on them, a small smile spread across her lips. Colten's tongue tied in knots. The cameras flipped to him, the crowd dashing away from their angles. She began to walk toward Dolly.

"This is Colten," she told the camera. "The one who made all this possible."

The crowd cheered a bit; someone whistled. But his eyes never left Ronnie.

"If you'll excuse me," she continued to tell the cameras, "I have a sunset to catch." She stopped in front of Dolly, petting her muzzle. "That is, if there's room for two up there?"

It'd been hard enough to let her leave the first time. Colten wasn't sure he could do it again. But he wasn't capable of telling her no, even knowing it could rip his heart into smaller pieces.

Colten hopped down from his horse. "What's all this?"

She shrugged. "My show. I told the producers the only way I'd agree to it was if they let me open my business in Starlight like I planned."

"You're staying?"

"Everything I want is in Starlight."

Colten removed his hat and dipped his chin to kiss Ronnie, thoughts of the cameras a faint concern. Sparks ignited all of his senses in that kiss. He heard a "Go, Colten!" from the crowd, and was unable to fight the smile that formed.

"I love you. No dream's complete without you in it, Colten."

He kissed her again, certain he made her toes curl. The crowd cheered around them, making them laugh. "The thought of living in that house without you was miserable. I love you, Ronnie. You're everything I've dreamed of and more."

"Better get going if we're going to catch that sunset."

Ronnie, looking right at home in her fitted jeans, nodded toward Dolly.

"We really need to work on your footwear,"

Colten teased as he mounted and held his hand out for Ronnie.

"What's wrong with my sandals?"

"Nothing." He shook his head in amusement at the crowd and the cameras, and let Dolly take them away. "Nothing at all."

EPILOGUE

Ronnie

Ronnie's first summer in Wyoming had been a busy one, but she wouldn't change a minute of it. Her new downtown office had opened for business. Clients were booked well into the winter months. Colten refused to let her work too many long hours, but knowing he was waiting for her at the end of the day helped her leave her work for the next day.

Dolly trotted up the familiar hill to their overlook point. Ronnie insisted Colten teach her to ride within a week of moving permanently to Starlight. She loved cozying up with him in the saddle, but she needed to feel as if she belonged, and that meant learning to ride solo.

As they neared the top of the hill, she asked Dolly, "What do you suppose is going on?"

Colten had asked her to meet him at their special spot just after sunset. At least that was all her brother had let on. Hudson had been the biggest surprise in all of this. He admitted to Ronnie that he'd figured out how she and Colten felt about each other before they ever did. "I can't imagine anyone better for my sister or my best friend." He shoved a jacket at her and ushered her out the door. "Now hurry up and get out there. He's waiting."

Dusk had given way to the night sky when Ronnie crested the hilltop. Dozens of twinkling flames danced in the gentle evening breeze, forming a perimeter around a fuzzy blanket. She slid off Dolly, catching Colten lighting a final candle.

"What is all this?"

Colten hopped up, hurrying to her side. He gathered her in his arms and kissed her until dizziness swept over her, and she found it hard to keep her footing on such weak legs. *Would it always be this way between them?* "Let me get Dolly situated. Go, have a seat."

Colten led her horse next to his own and tied the reins.

Ronnie kicked off her sandals, leaving them at the edge of the blanket. The candles, she noticed, were a couple of feet from the edge, but their silhouette made the setting truly magical. She dropped onto the blanket, stretching out her legs and leaning back to admire the millions of stars painting the sky above. She *lived* here! Sometimes it still felt like a dream. "I am never going to get tired of this amazing view!"

"Neither am I." Colten was beside her, propped on one knee.

Ronnie couldn't breathe at the sight of her irritatingly handsome cowboy kneeling, a velvet box outstretched.

"Ronnie Ross, you've been on my mind since the second you crashed into me."

"Hey!"

A mischievous smirk formed. "Shh. I'm proposing." Ronnie found she couldn't speak. "I thought you were sent here to drive me crazy, and it turns out I was right. You drive me crazy every time I see your smile. You drive me crazy every time you kiss me. You even drive me crazy in those ridiculous wedges."

Ronnie laughed, swiping away a tear. "They're pretty amazing shoes." Would he just ask the question already so she could kiss him?

"Ronnie, I love you with every beat of my heart. Please tell me you'll drive me crazy for the rest of my life. Will you marry me?"

"Yes!" Her left hand trembled as Colten slipped the most beautiful diamond ring she'd ever seen onto her finger. The moment it was on, Ronnie threw her arms around his neck and kissed him deeply. The passionate kiss rolled them onto the blanket. Ronnie curled against his chest as his arm went around her. Together, they stared up at the star-filled sky.

"I love you, Colten Livingston." Ronnie had never been happier. What could be better than cozying up next to the man she loved—the man she'd just agreed to spend the rest of her life with—as they watched the stars dance in the vast Wyoming sky? The man who held her in his arms had made all her dreams come true.

~THE END~

Sign up for Jacqueline Winter's newsletter to receive alerts about current projects and new releases!

http://eepurl.com/du18iz

COMING SOON

Cowboys & Firelight - A Starlight Sweet Romance
Book 2

Cowboys & Moonlight - A Starlight Sweet Romance
Book 3

ABOUT THE AUTHOR

Jacqueline Winters has been writing since she was nine when she'd sneak stacks of paper from her grandma's closet and fill them with adventure. She grew up in small-town Nebraska and spent a decade living in beautiful Alaska. She writes sweet contemporary romance and contemporary romantic suspense.

She's a sucker for happily ever afters, has a sweet tooth that can be sated with cupcakes, and believes sangria was possibly the best invention ever. On a relaxing evening, you can find her at her computer writing her next novel with her faithful dog poking his adorable head out from beneath her desk.

facebook.com/JacquelineWintersRomance

goodreads.com/jacquelinewinters

ACKNOWLEDGMENTS

To Nikki – the first one who cheered me on when I monopolized hours of Skype conversations to talk about my new series and writing goals. Thank you for never once calling me crazy!

To Mom – the biggest cheerleader in my corner. Thank you for reminding me daily to keep going because I'm already in the process of living my dream.

To Dad – I wish I'd had the chance to tell you about my new goals as a writer. I think you would have been my biggest supporter. I hope I'm making you proud.

To my critiquers – Nikki, Jen, Jessica, Kristin, Barb – Thank you for your flexibility and, as always, your invaluable feedback.

To my editor EJ – the best story coach I know.

Thank you for teaching me how to make my story come alive on the page.

To my copy editor Brenda – I always get giddy when I see how your touch makes my story shine.

To my proofreader Michelle – Thank you for being the final set of eyes.

To my cover artist Victorine – There were tears of joy the first time I saw this cover. Thank you for creating such a beautiful design!

To the Writing Gals – Thank you for sharing your wealth of knowledge. I'm so happy to have stumbled onto such an amazing group of uplifting writers.

Made in the USA
San Bernardino, CA
09 March 2020